# LI
# THE FIRST STAGES



To: MR. & Mrs. Cook! & Julia
Best Wishes!
Michelle Cole

## MICHELLE COLE

**Write World**
**"we write the books that make the whole world read!"™**

Write World Publishing Group, Inc.
3523 McKinney Avenue Suite # 373
Dallas, Texas 75204



Library of Congress Control Number: 2002108466

Cole, Michelle
Lilla belle the first stages / Michelle Cole

ISBN 0-9722173-0-4

Manufactured in the United States of America

Published simultaneously in Canada

December 2002

*"This book is dedicated to the precious jewels of our future... children."*

*-Michelle Cole*

# FROM THE MOMENT

From the moment that I became a mother, I vowed to teach her, guide her, and love her.
From the moment I held her in my arms, I knew I would meet death, before I let her meet harm.
From the moment I looked into her eyes, I beamed with pride, they looked just like mine.
From the moment she spoke her very first word, it was the most beautiful voice I had ever heard.
From the moment that she took her first step, overwhelmed with joy, I cheered and wept.
From the moment I saw her watching me, I led by example, by showing her, how she should be.
From the moment I saw her married, with children of her own, I couldn't believe it! Where had all the years gone?
From the moment I saw that healthy lady, I thanked God that I raised, that healthy baby!

* * * * *

*A very special thanks to my first and most important teachers: Lamar and Lillie Cole*

*-all my love,*

*M.*

# LILLA BELLE
## THE FIRST STAGES

Table of Contents:

## *Chapter One*
## **The Mummies**

"Lilla Belle! Lilla Belle! Time to get up, honey!" Mrs. Wongley yelled excitedly. "It's your first day of school! Lilla Belle?"

Lea Wongley knew something was wrong. Her daughter was a light sleeper. Lilla Belle had been a light sleeper since birth. Lea remembered how she, her husband, Benjamin, and their then two-year-old son, Zachari, would have to be really quiet whenever Lilla Belle fell asleep. Even slight sounds would awaken her.

"I'm sick, Mommie, I feel awful," Lilla Belle replied, frowning.

"Oh, sweetheart," said her mother, as she felt Lilla Belle's forehead. "It doesn't feel like you have a fever. What's wrong?"

Lilla Belle tried to remember what her brother, Zach, had last year. Mom had kept him home from school. M? M...? Lilla Belle thought... It started with an m. Mum...? Gosh! I can't remember. The little girl looked frustrated.

"Mommie, I have the mummies," said Lilla Belle, finally.

Her mother looked puzzled. "You have the what?" Lea Wongley asked her daughter.

"I have the mummies!" Lilla Belle said again, trying to sound much more convincing this time. She looked at her mother with those big, pretty, dark eyes.

"Lilla Belle, I'm thirty-five years old, and I have never heard of such. The only mummies that I've ever seen are the ones on TV and in the movies, but they are not real. Lilla Belle, you're certainly not a mummy."

"Maybe I'm not pronouncing it correctly. It's whatever Zach had last year," Lilla Belle insisted.

Her mother laughed. "Your brother had the 'mumps' last year, Lilla Belle, not the mummies! You don't have the mumps either. Believe me, if you had the mumps, I'd know. Sweetheart, what is this REALLY about?"

"Mom!" Zach called from his bedroom. "Mom!"

"I'll be right back, Lilla Belle," Lea Wongley told her daughter.

A few minutes after her mother left the room, Lilla Belle jumped out of bed and started dancing around and singing. "I'm not going to school today. I'm not going to school today. I'm not..."

She stopped singing and dancing after spotting her parents, who were standing by her bedroom door, watching her.

"Uh-oh. I've blown it now," said Lilla Belle, looking upset.

"Uh-oh is right," her father said.

Lea Wongley stood, looking at their daughter, curiously. "Your 'mummies,' healed very quickly, young lady."

"Indeed they did," said her father.

Benjamin Wongley took the morning off to take his daughter to school. This was Lilla Belle's first day of school, and he wanted to be there.

"Ben," as most people called him, was President and CEO of Wongley Inc., a Fortune 500 company.

Benjamin Wongley was a very successful businessman. He was also a very respectable one. Ben's family was second in his life only to God. His business ranked third. Everyone knew how important Ben's family was to him.

"Young lady, you have some explaining to do," said her father.

Tears welled up in Lilla Belle's eyes. "Mommie, Daddy, I don't want to go to school. I was really excited at first. I love all of my new school clothes and all, but..."

"But what, Lilla Belle? What's changed your mind? What is it?" her mother asked. "You know that you can talk to us, sweetheart, about anything."

"I, I'm just scared to be without you and Daddy and Zach. I don't want to be left alone with a roomful of people that I don't know," said Lilla Belle, looking at her parents the same way she did when she wanted to get them to change their minds.

Ben Wongley picked up his little girl. He sat Lilla Belle on her bed and wiped her tears. Ben remembered how he felt, many years ago, when it was his first day of school. He had also cried.

"Sweetheart, going to school is not an option. You and Zach are going to the same school. He will be in a different class though, because he's older than you, but he'll still be there," her father explained.

Lea looked at her daughter. "I have an idea! Let's sing 'your' song. On the count of three. One-eee... Two-ooo... Three-eee..."

Lilla Belle and her father joined in.

***"Lil-la Belle! Lil-la Belle! She's the bravest little girl in the whole wide world! Whole wide world! With a heart so big and a smile so bright; no matter what happens she will stand by your side! Lil-la Belle! Lil-la Belle! With long black hair, and eyes that shine, she's pretty as can be and she's oh so wise! Lil-la Belle! Lil-la Belle!"***

Lea Wongley was happy to see her daughter smiling again. That song always made Lilla Belle feel better. Lea had been singing that song to her daughter since she'd first brought her home from the hospital. The entire Wongley family knew the song by heart.

No one loved the song more than Lilla Belle. Her dark eyes would always light up, whenever her mother would sing that song to her.

"You know who else is going to be there?" Lea Wongley asked her daughter.

Before Lilla Belle could answer, Zach broke in, "Ivana! Ivana will be there, Lilla Belle." Ivana and Lilla Belle were best friends.

After eavesdropping, Zach felt he had to do whatever he could to make his little sister feel better. He knew that she had been crying, and Zach hated to see his sister cry.

Lilla Belle and Zach were close, although they would argue and tease one another sometimes. Zach loved his little sister. He was very protective of her, too.

****

The fact that her best friend was going to be in her class made Lilla Belle feel much better.

"Really?" asked Lilla Belle. "Is Ivana really going to the same school? Are we going to be in the same class?"

"You sure are!" said her mother.

"And speaking of class, we'd better get going! You don't want to be late on your first day of school, Lilla Belle," said her father.

As Lilla Belle took her bath, brushed her teeth, and dressed for school, she thought about what Grandma Ella had told her and Zach last summer.

"Change can be good," she had told them.

"Change can be good," Lilla Belle said aloud.

After Mrs. Wongley finished brushing and combing Lilla Belle's hair, the doorbell rang. That must be Dolores and Ivana, Lea thought. She'd seen Jack, Dolores's husband, leave earlier that morning.

The Wrights lived down the street from the Wongleys. They were close neighbors. Ben and Jack would often go fishing and play golf together. Lea and Dolores did some things together, too. They especially loved going shopping at Neiman Marcus.

Before unlocking the door, Zach performed his usual routine; he looked through the peephole, first. It was a safety measure his parents taught him and his sister.

"It's Mrs. Wright and Ivana!" said Zach, as he opened the door to let their neighbors in.

"Good morning, all!" said the usually vibrant Dolores Wright. "My! You're looking awfully pretty, Lilla Belle."

****

"Thank you, Mrs. Wright," said Lilla Belle, smiling.

Lilla Belle was beautiful! She had big, pretty, dark eyes, a smile that lit up any room, and long, curly, black hair that fell well below her shoulders.

"Ivana, you look pretty, too," said Mrs. Wongley, as she smiled at her daughter's best friend.

"And speaking of looks, you're looking awfully handsome, Zach," both ladies said in unison.

"Thanks!" said Zach, as he hurried upstairs to get his backpack.

"Are you excited?" Lilla Belle asked Ivana.

"I'm actually more nervous," said Ivana. "I'm also a little..."

"Scared?" Lilla Belle asked Ivana.

"Yes," said Ivana. "I am scared."

"Don't worry! Change can be good," said Lilla Belle, trying to make her best friend feel better.

Lea and Dolores looked at each other, marveling at what Lilla Belle had just said.

"Five going on fifty," said Lea Wongley, shaking her head.

"Grandma Ella told me that," said Lilla Belle.

"Well, Mother's right, change can be good."

And on that note, it was time to go, time to head to Jones Elementary School. Jones was a very prestigious public school. The school was just five miles away from Beaver Creek, where the Wongleys and Wrights resided.

"We're here!" said Ben Wongley, pulling into the school's parking lot, minutes later.

****

Zach was taken to class first. The Wongleys and Mrs. Wright met his teacher, Mrs. Elnora Marcus; then they went to take the girls to their class.

"Room 120, Miss Betty Monner," said Lea Wongley, reading the sign above the door. "Here we are!"

As they entered the kindergarten class, they were greeted immediately by a little girl who seemed very excited.

"Hi, there!" said the little girl, staring at them.

"Hello!" they all said, as the teacher approached them.

"Hello, I'm Miss Monner," said the teacher, extending her hand.

"Nice to meet you, Miss Monner," said the parents, shaking the teacher's hand and introducing themselves.

"Well, girls, it looks like the only empty desks left are in the front," said Lea Wongley, trying to sound upbeat.

After walking the girls to their desks and giving them a big hug and kiss, Ben, Lea, and Dolores left.

As they walked to the car, Ben looked at the ladies and shook his head. "I had to get you two out of there. Look at both of you!" he told them, referring to the tears in their eyes. "The girls will be just fine. Lea, we went through this two years ago when Zach started school."

"I know, but it still didn't make it any easier," said Lea.

****

“Good morning, class! I’m your teacher. My name is Miss Monner.” The teacher smiled. “Welcome! I would like each of you to stand up and introduce yourselves. Simply tell us your first and last name. Okay? We will start with you, young lady,” said the teacher, pointing at Lilla Belle.

Lilla Belle stood up. “My name is Lilla Belle Wongley.”

“My name is Ivana Wright.”

“My name is Shemara Washington. My aunt calls me ‘Mara’! You’ll can call me Mara, too!”

So that was the little girl’s name who had greeted them when they first walked in. She certainly doesn’t seem nervous, thought Lilla Belle, as she sized up Shemara. She’s pretty, too. A little too thin, nice hair, friendly, nice smile, pretty name. Lilla Belle finally turned her attention back to the other students.

As each student stood up and said his or her name, Miss Monner checked off each name, making sure that everyone was present.

“Great!” said Miss Monner, closing her roll call book. “Every morning, one of the first things I will do is take roll call. This just means when I call your name, you simply respond by saying, ‘here.’ Also, while I am speaking, if any of you has questions, please raise your hand. Now, today is a very special day. Your first day of school will always be one of your most memorable, too. School is a very important and beneficial part of life.”

Mara smiled and raised her hand.

“Yes, Miss Washington?” the teacher asked.

“Will we have any homework today?” Mara asked Miss Monner.

****

Miss Monner shook her head and laughed. "No, I will not assign any homework today. Since today is your first day, I will go easy on you. Before I continue, does anyone else have any questions at this time?" the teacher asked. "Anyone?" she asked again. Miss Monner went on. "Education is the first priority and main reason for going to school. School is also a great place to meet people and make new friends. During your first year of school, you will learn how to write your name, how to count, the alphabet, and how to form words using the alphabet. You will also learn some very fun songs!" Miss Monner smiled before continuing. "Art, coloring, tracing objects, how to use scissors properly... the list goes on," said the teacher. "I am here to help each of you."

Lilla Belle and Ivana exchanged looks. The two best friends smiled at each other. Maybe this wasn't going to be so bad after all, they both thought.

The rest of the day was spent going to recess, going to lunch, napping, and learning new songs.

After waking from their nap, Miss Monner gave each of the children a snack. During snack time, the teacher read several books to the class.

The girls had a fun-filled first day. When the school bell rang to go home, both girls told Mrs. Wongley, who was waiting for them in the hallway, what a great day they'd had.

"I can't wait to come back tomorrow!" said Lilla Belle.

"Tomorrow is Saturday," Zach told his sister.

"Aw!" said Lilla Belle, as she got in the car.

****

"How was your day, Zach?" Lea Wongley asked her son.

"Great, Mom. I had fun, too! There are three new kids in my class who weren't there last year."

"Who?" his sister asked.

"Cameron, Andriayna, and Malik. And guess what? They are all first cousins!" said Zach, before anyone else could answer. "Isn't that something?" Zach asked his mother.

"Yes, Zach, it sure is."

A short time later, they were in the Wrights' driveway dropping Ivana off.

"Hi, there!" Dolores said, greeting them and hugging her daughter. "My, looks like your first day of school was a lot of fun."

"It was, Mom. Lilla Belle and I had a whole lot of fun! Our teacher is really, really nice, too," Ivana said, happily, as her big blue eyes lit up.

"I'm so glad to hear that. I told both of you that everything would be fine," said Dolores.

"We told them," said Lea Wongley, smiling.

"Thanks, Lea. Have a great weekend!" said Dolores.

"You, too, Dee. Call me! 'Bye, Ivana!" said Lea Wongley. "Any homework?" she asked her kids.

"I don't have any," Zach said.

"I don't either," said Lilla Belle. "Miss Monner said that she would go easy on us, since today was our first day of school."

"I see," said Lea Wongley. "Lilla Belle, the rule of thumb is homework first, BEFORE television. Always! Your brother already knows that. We will leave in an hour for practice. You two go change clothes."

****

Four days each week, Mrs. Wongley, Zach, and Lilla Belle went to martial arts class.

At the age of thirty-six, Benjamin Wongley retired as the undefeated world champion in both taekwondo, (a Korean martial art) and jujitsu (an ancient Japanese martial art that gives a small man a decided advantage over a larger opponent.) Ben kept his martial arts skills sharp by practicing regularly.

The rest of the Wongley clan also studied and practiced taekwondo and jujitsu. They attended Ching's Five Star Martial Arts Academy.

"The essence of traditional jujitsu is that you should use the energy and strength of your opponent and turn it against him," Master Ching told them on the first day. "Jujitsu is a very elusive form of martial arts. Elusive means to avoid being captured," said Master Ching, while giving his students numerous demonstrations.

Lee Ching taught the adults' class. His brother, Zuang Ching, taught the children's class.

Master Ching, or "sensei," as students called their martial arts teacher, began class with his usual reminder. "There are numerous benefits gained from studying and practicing martial arts, besides self-defense: respect, discipline, self-esteem, and self-confidence."

Lilla Belle approached Master Ching after class. "Sensei, my parents told my brother and me that parents are a child's first teacher."

"That is correct, Wise-one, parents are also a child's most important teacher," said Master Ching, smiling.

Class was very enjoyable and a good learning tool for the children as usual.

On the way home from practice, Mrs. Wongley took Lilla Belle and Zach to Baskin Robbins for ice cream.

"Tonight is family night!" Lilla Belle said, excitedly.

"That's right," said her mother.

Friday night was family night at the Wongleys. This was the one night that the entire family would spend time doing something together, as a family.

Sometimes they would pair up to play board games, watch a couple of movies at home, or go out to dinner and to the movies afterwards.

Regardless of what the Wongleys decided to do on family night, it was a night they all looked forward to and enjoyed.

There was an unanimous vote that each of them would rent one movie from Blockbuster.

"We have popcorn, right?" Benjamin Wongley asked his family.

"Yes," Lea Wongley replied. "I bought some yesterday when I went to the grocery store."

"Great, then we're all set!" said Ben.

During dinner that evening, the Wongleys enjoyed great food and good conversation. Afterwards, they settled down for a nice, quiet evening at home, watching movies and eating popcorn.

*Chapter Two*
**The Weekend**

Early the next morning, the phone rang. It was Lea's sister Sylvia, whom she called, "Sister Travis."

"Hello, Sister Travis," said Lea, yawning.

"Did I wake you, Lea?"

"Yes, but that's okay. We all went to bed pretty late last night. Ben and the kids are still sleeping. How are you doing?" Lea asked her sister.

"I'm doing fine," said Sylvia. "How are you'll doing?"

"We're doing fine. The kids are getting bigger every day," said Lea.

"Can I pick the kids up later today?" Sylvia asked. "I'm going to the fair and I'd like to take Lilla Belle and Zach. I'm sure they'll like that."

"Oh, yes! I'm sure they will, too. What time did you want to pick them up?" Lea asked.

"Around noonish."

"They will be ready," Lea told her sister.

"They are going to have a ball!" said Sylvia. "I heard the fair has even more rides this year."

Lea decided to go downstairs and make coffee. She knew that she was going to be on the phone with her sister for a good while, and she didn't want to wake Ben and the kids. Several hours later, Sylvia finally said good-bye.

When Lea heard footsteps upstairs, she started making breakfast.

After breakfast, everyone pitched in to help clean the kitchen. Then, for Lilla Belle and Zach, it was chore time.

Two hours later, Zach called from upstairs. "Mom! We're finished with all of our chores!"

"Okay, start getting ready. Aunt Sylvia will be here soon," his mother replied.

****

"Good-bye, kids!" Ben and Lea stood, waving from their front door. "Have a great time! Be good!"

Shortly after Ben closed the door, the doorbell rang. Ben looked through the peephole. "It's Miss Flossy."

Oh, boy, Lea Wongley thought. Miss Flossy and her husband lived two doors down from the Wrights. Though married, she insisted everyone call her "Miss" Flossy, instead of "Mrs." Flossy. And Miss Flossy, well, she was simply, Miss Flossy. She would say exactly what she thought about anything, or anyone for that matter, thus earning her the nickname, "Miss Tell It Like It T.I. Is Flossy." She would watch what she'd say around the children though. The Wongleys wouldn't have it any other way.

"She has a martial arts uniform on," Ben whispered to his wife, as he opened the door, reluctantly. "Hi, Miss Flossy."

"Hi, Miss Flossy." The elderly lady mocked Ben. "You ain't gotta look so happy to see me. You will be ol' one day. And I guarantee ya, you'll be knockin' at the door of somebody. Or should I say somebody's door? You betta hope they letcha in, Ben. Anyway, I sho' do hope that I wasn't disturbin' anythang," said Miss Flossy, inviting herself in. "And, Ben, you may wanna learn to whisper a little lower next time. I heard everythang you said."

"Well, actually..." Ben didn't finish his sentence.

Miss Flossy headed for the kitchen. "Lea, child, I gotta talk to you! Can I have a cup of coffee?"

"Sure, Miss Flossy," said Lea.

"I'll be in my office, honey," Ben told his wife, bending down to kiss her on the cheek. "Nice seeing you again, Miss Flossy."

"You, too, Ben. You, too. Girl! You are so lucky. That Ben Wongley makes a ol' woman wish for younga days! He sho' is a handsome devil. Don't tell Alvin I said that either," said Miss Flossy, laughing. Alvin Booker was Miss Flossy's husband of fifty-five years. "Ben is certainly lucky to have you, too. You two make a great couple! And I ain't just talkin' 'bout looks either."

"Thank you," said Lea, as she looked at the elderly woman, who was the biggest gossiper in town.

Miss Flossy was ninety years old. She was a very petite woman with a toothless grin. Her long white hair was as white as snow. She had tiny dark eyes that reminded Lea of an eagle's eyes. They watched you like a hawk. Miss Flossy's vision was still good, too. She was also very alert. Lea Wongley watched her with quiet amusement.

Miss Flossy never ceased to surprise her. Lea had never heard her say anything about taking martial arts.

"What 'cha lookin' at me like that fo'? Am I too ol' to take karate?" Miss Flossy asked, as if reading Lea's mind.

"No, ma'am," said Lea quickly. "Not at all."

"Tell me somethin'! You never too ol' to learn." Lea nodded her head in agreement. "Didn't yo' momma ever tell you that?" Miss Flossy laughed hard. "Child, you and Ben know I'm just teasin' you'll. I love to tease. This ol' pretty lady don't mean nobody no harm."

The Wongleys had known Miss Flossy for years. Ben and Lea were used to her teasing and her bluntness. If one ever wanted to laugh, she was the person to call.

"How have you been doing, Miss Flossy?" Lea asked.

"Child, I'm sho' glad you asked! That ol' devil sho' is busy. My pastor tell us all the time to resist the devil, and he'll flee from you. Well, apparently my resistance ain't too strong!" said Miss Flossy. Lea laughed. She could hear Ben laughing, too. It was very hard not to laugh at Miss Flossy. "I'm serious, child!" Miss Flossy took a sip of her coffee. "Child, we have a famous psychic. Haven't you heard?"

"Who?" Lea Wongley asked. "Miss Cleo?"

"Naw, child, Sister Leo! I found out just yesterday that she makes money posin' as a phone psychic. Sister Leo ain't bit more a psychic than a man in a moon. If Marcy Leo's a psychic, I'm a astronaut. And, child, as ol' as I am, not to mention, my fear of flyin', you know that I ain't no moon person. If I was gonna go to the moon, I would be so scared that I would lose the one tooth that I got left!" Lea laughed hard. "That would be one truly heart stoppin' experience. And it would also be the end of ol' Flossy!" Miss Flossy sipped her coffee. "Now, Lea, you probably don't remember me tellin' you that Sister Leo stood up in church several months ago, sayin' that she was worried about her bills. She say if somethin' didn't happen soon, she was gonna do somethin' drastic. And soon, child. Well, looks like she a woman of her word. I would never have pictured her a psychic. A psycho maybe, but not a psychic, child! From what I hear, she's rakin' in green! And lots of it, too, child. That explains that new Benz that she's drivin'. She claims it's her daughter's. She done struck gold, child!" Miss Flossy took another sip of her coffee. "And just how many offerings is that new pastor of mine's gonna take up? He take up no less than seven offerings every Sunday. What in heaven's name fo'?" The old lady sipped her coffee again. "Well, I guess fo' that newly built mansion, those three BMWs, that Benz, that caddy, and that Lexus coupe. I guess that should answer the question, and answer it with a quickness, too, child! You haven't seen my pastor's house?" Lea shook her head no. "Well, child, let me tell you, his house looks like somethin' outta those very rich and famous magazines. No harm, but his house looks like this one. And, somethin' like my own." Miss Flossy was a very rich woman. She and her husband had made a fortune in the stock market. Miss Flossy had also been a very shrewd and successful businesswoman. "Child, let me tell you, my pastor is always preachin' on prosperity; the only one who seems to be prosperin' is him." Miss Flossy laughed. "Well, I'm sho' glad I ain't gotta worry about money. You don't either, child. You ain't gotta tell me. I know you don't! You'll own just about everythang in Beaver Creek. They should rename our town Wongley Creek." Miss Flossy flashed a toothless grin. "How's Monica doin' in Oakland, or as the young folks say, Oaktown?"

"Monica's doing great. Her son is doing fine, too. She loves California," said Lea.

"Now, I already know how your other sister's doin'. Shevette's still not doin' too well, is she?" Miss Flossy flashed a toothless grin.

"Shevette is fine," said Lea. Shevette, as everyone knew, was never doing too well.

"How's Sylvia doin'?" Miss Flossy asked.

"Sylvia is doing great," said Lea. "She took the children to the fair."

"And Gwendolyn?"

"Gwen is fine, too. She's living in Fort Worth now," Lea replied.

"Good! Okay, now, gettin' to tha question that I really want a answer to. Does Lamar and Loredo still have a crush on me?" Miss Flossy asked.

"A crush on you?" asked Lea.

"Now, Lea, I know you ain't no slow woman. You know what I mean. They thank I'm cute."

Lea shrugged her shoulders. "I don't know, Miss Flossy."

"Child, I'm the picture of fitness: martial arts, joggin' five miles a day, drinkin' lots and lots of water, and watchin' my intake. You know I gots to watch my girlish figure! I'm the picture of beauty, too, child!"

"You jog five miles a day?" Lea was impressed.

"In my dreams, child!" Miss Flossy flashed another toothless grin. "You cain't knock a woman for dreamin'. Child, I cain't even walk down the street without near cardiac arrest!"

Lea laughed. "How long have you been taking martial arts, Miss Flossy?"

Miss Flossy grinned. "Long enough to knock the day and night lights out of somebody, if they mess with me, that's how long! After hearin' 'bout all of those pretty, 'mature' ladies being grabbed, ol' Flossy decided to spring into action! As cute as I am, I know all eyes are on me anyway, so I gots to protect myself. The way I look, child, I'd be foolish not to. But I have one guarantee that they can count on," said Miss Flossy.

"Guarantee?" Lea Wongley asked.

"Yeah, child. If anyone grabs me, I guarantee you, that they will let me go, just as quickly as they grabbed me. Child, I'm ready! I'm so bad, I scare myself. Let me tell you! Not sometimes, all the time, child. I am bad with a capital bumblebee. And honey, listen, I make moves, not fake moves!" Miss Flossy flashed another toothless grin, as she talked, and talked, and talked... "Oh, my! Look at tha time! Ol' Flossy gots to go! Child, I must say, as always, it was a pleasure talkin' to you. Kiss those beautiful kids fo' me."

"I'll do that," Lea Wongley assured her.

"You have company," said Miss Flossy, as she stood in the Wongleys' front yard.

Who could it be? Lea Wongley wondered. They were not expecting any company. Lea looked out the window. She smiled as soon as she saw who it was.

When Miss Flossy saw who it was, she flashed a toothless grin. "I think I'll stay just a little while longer. You don't mind, Lea, do ya?"

"Not at all, Miss Flossy," said Lea.

Miss Flossy grinned. "Thanks. I'll go freshen up!" She immediately went to the Wongleys' guest bathroom to brush her hair and put on lipstick.

"Lamar and Loredo! Ben, your brothers are here!" Lea called from downstairs, as she walked outside to greet her husband's brothers.

"How's our sister doing?" Lamar asked, giving Lea a hug.

"I'm fine, Lamar, how are you? Hello, Loredo!" said Lea.

"Where's my hug?" Miss Flossy asked the two men, as she smiled and batted her eyelashes. Lamar and Loredo blushed as they gave Miss Flossy a hug.

Miss Flossy smiled at Lea and winked her eye. "Told ya," she whispered.

"We decided to drive down and pay our family a little visit. Where is that brother of ours?" Lamar asked.

"Hey! What's up?" said Ben, as he gave each of his brothers a big hug.

"Where are the kids?" Loredo asked.

"Sylvia took them to the fair," said Ben.

"Make yourselves comfortable. Have a seat. Can I get anyone anything?" Lea Wongley asked.

"Oh, no, thank you. We stopped by Golden Corral on our way here," Lamar told Lea.

"I'll have another cup of 'fresh' coffee. Thanks," said Miss Flossy.

"Sure," said Lea Wongley.

"How is the rest of the family?" Ben asked his brothers.

"Everyone is doing just fine," Loredo answered. Time passed quickly as everyone talked about past and present events.

Ben and Lea were surprised to find Miss Flossy still there.

"It's getting late, Loredo. We'd better get going. I can't spend the night," Lamar joked. "I have to get back home to Lillie Mae!"

"Yeah, we'd better ease on down the road. I have to get back home to Catherine, too. I also have a photo shoot tonight," said Loredo.

Miss Flossy cleared her throat. "Gentlemen, if I could have just a few more minutes of your time, please."

Ben and Lea exchanged looks. Miss Flossy spoke impeccable English. They only laughed and shook their heads. Miss Flossy was full of surprises.

Miss Flossy went on, "I'd like to demonstrate a martial arts technique that I learned in class. Who would like to be lying on their back, looking up at the ceiling?" Her beety eyes stopped on Lamar. "How 'bout it, Mr. Lamar? You been laughin' at me in my uniform since you got here."

The Wongleys exchanged looks again, back to "Flossy language," they both thought.

"Miss Flossy, really, I wasn't laughing at you. I was laughing with you," said Lamar.

"How was you laughin' with me when I wasn't even laughin'? You scared? Chicken?" Miss Flossy flapped both of her arms.

"No, ma'am, I'm not scared," Lamar replied.

"Well, as the young folks say, bring it on! I ain't MC Hammer, but let's get it started!" Miss Flossy quipped.

"We really have to go, Miss Flossy," said Lamar, who looked at Loredo for help.

"Well, actually, Lamar, we have time," said Loredo.

Everyone followed Miss Flossy and Lamar into the Wongleys' gym, which was state of the art. The mats were already in place from Ben practicing the day before.

"I won't be long, Lamar. I ain't got a lot of time either. I'll just flip ya, then send ya back to that beautiful wife of yours," said Miss Flossy.

All eyes were on Miss Flossy and Lamar. Within seconds, Lamar was on his back looking up at the ceiling.

True to her word, Miss Flossy had flipped Lamar like a rag doll.

Everyone stood amazed. The petite and fragile looking lady was as tough as nails.

Miss Flossy flashed a toothless grin. "Never judge a book by its cover!" said Miss Flossy, as she bid everyone farewell. "Now, my work for today is done. Ol' Flossy gots to go! See ya! Wouldn't want to be ya, Lamar!"

Ben held up one hand. "Lamar? How many fingers do you see?" Everyone laughed, except Lamar. "I have to tell a long list of people about this! Tiny, Harry, Ida Mae, Stanley, Bill, Tori, Tommy, Melvin, Ophelia, Robert Dean, Edna, Reginald, Debbie, Edith, George, Shane, Sedric, Mark, and Vicky." Ben looked at his wife. "Sweetheart, did I miss anyone?"

Lea Wongley only smiled in answer. She was still in shock. Lamar, flipped by an elderly lady. Lea shook her head in amazement. Unbelievable! Miss Flossy was very good at karate. She'd definitely made a believer out of her. Out of all of us, thought Lea, still shaking her head.

Loredo laughed. "Ben, don't worry; I will be sure to tell everyone you left out. Everyone is going to know about this! And I do mean everyone."

"Everyone, hush! Just hush!" said Lamar. "That was simply luck. The old lady got lucky, that's all. Well, actually, I let her flip me. I made it easy for her. Now, c'mon, how would I look flipping a lady that's two hundred years old? You all know me better than that. Let's go, Loredo!"

"Lamar, I know some very good chiropractors," Ben joked.

"I do mean to be rude when I say, Ben, shut up!" said Lamar.

Ben shook his head. "My brother, ol' tough Lamar, flipped by an elderly lady! 'Bye guys. Be careful!"

****

Lilla Belle and Zach arrived home a short time later.

"You'll just missed Uncle Lamar and Uncle Loredo," their father told them, "not to mention a great martial arts demonstration."

"Demonstration? You and Uncle Jesse?" Zach asked.

His father laughed. "No, Son, Miss Flossy and Uncle Lamar."

"Really?" said Lilla Belle and Zach in unison.

"Miss Flossy knows martial arts?" Zach asked.

"Apparently, Son."

"Wow!" Zach replied.

"Cool!" said Lilla Belle. "We women are awesome!"

After Lilla Belle and Zach took their baths, they were out like a light.

"What a day they must have had," said Lea Wongley.

"No kidding!" said Ben, carrying the children one by one upstairs to their bedrooms.

Shortly after putting the kids to bed, Lea could hear Ben singing in the shower. That was usually the only time her husband would sing. He didn't sing too badly. Then again, he didn't sing too well either, Lea thought, laughing.

Before going to bed that night, Mr. and Mrs. Wongley went to check on their children as they usually did before turning in themselves. Lilla Belle and Zach were both sleeping soundly.

Afterwards, Ben and Lea said their prayers and climbed into bed.

"Good night, honey," Lea said, giving her husband a kiss. "Sweet dreams."

"Good night, sweetheart."

The phone rang.

"It's probably your brothers. I asked them to call us when they made it home," Lea told her husband.

Ben answered the phone. "Hello."

"We made it," said Lamar. "Love to all!"

"Even Miss Flossy?" Ben asked. There was an immediate dial tone. Lamar hung up on his brother. Ben laughed as he told his wife. "I guess the jokes are getting to him, but we're not joking. It's true. Lamar was flipped by a ninety-year-old woman, and I will never let him live it down. Never! That old lady packs a punch, doesn't she?"

"Oh, yes! We all know that now. Miss Flossy wasn't just talking today. She showed all of us that she is more than capable of taking care of business. I feel very sorry for whomever tries to do anything to her. They will be in for a big surprise," said Lea Wongley.

"A very rude awakening!" Ben agreed.

****

## *Chapter Three*
## **Parent-Child Conference**

The next day, after the Wongleys came home from church and changed clothes, the foursome sat in the living room to have their usual parent-child conference. This was something that Ben and Lea Wongley consistently did with their children. As **parents**, they knew how important it was to **talk to**, **and listen to**, their **children**. Ben and Lea knew that open lines of communication were vital.

The Wongleys would talk about issues that were important to both parent and child, and they would also discuss in depth, good and bad things that were happening in the world.

Lilla Belle and Zach could ask their parents anything they wanted to ask them, and their parents encouraged them to ask questions.

During the Wongley conference, there were no interruptions. There were no time limits either.

"Okay, Lilla Belle and Zach, we all know the rules. No interrupting anyone," said their father.

"Everyone will be heard; no one will be ignored. And remember, there are no stupid questions. Your father and I want you to ask questions. We want you to talk to us. We care about your feelings. And we want to know what's on your minds," said Lea Wongley.

Ben and Lea had a great relationship with their children, and they were determined to keep it that way. They wanted Lilla Belle and Zach to know that they could talk to them about anything.

"We love both of you very much, and as parents, our responsibility isn't just providing for you financially, it's also providing that which money cannot buy: unconditional love, parental guidance, support, discipline, teaching you great morals and values. We want you to be people with integrity, people with character. **Early teaching is** crucial. It's **very important**. It's never too early to teach, nor is it ever too early to learn. Lilla Belle, do you remember what morals, values, and integrity mean?" her father asked.

"Morals, values, and integrity?" Her father nodded. "Morals are the principles of right and wrong. When a person has great morals, they will do what is right. And values," Lilla Belle paused, "I know that when a person values anything, it means that it is important to them, usually very important. When you value something, you have a high regard for it, or in some cases, someone." Her parents nodded. "Integrity. When you are a person with integrity, you are determined to do what's right. There are no shades of gray. Morals, values, and integrity, all boil down to doing what is right. Did I ramble?"

"Sweetheart, you did just fine. Great memory, Lilla Belle," said her father. "Excellent!" Lilla Belle smiled.

"Lilla Belle, you told Master Ching that parents are a child's first teacher. You remember Ben and I telling you that. I'm proud of you, Lilla Belle. That tells me that you're listening." Lea looked at her son. "And, Zach, from what I can see, you are also listening. I'm very proud of both of you. But, more important than listening, is applying what you know. If you don't use what you know, having the knowledge is meaningless and useless. Knowledge and know-how won't help you, unless you use it. Show what you know; use what you know. I want our teachings to stick with both of you, now and always, no matter where you are. And no matter who you're with." Lilla Belle and Zach nodded. "We're going to talk about a number of topics today. They are all very important. And they are never to be taken lightly. First on the agenda. Drugs. Lilla Belle, should you use drugs?"

"No way!" said Lilla Belle.

"Lilla Belle, why not? Why shouldn't you use drugs?" her father asked. All eyes were on the little girl, as her parents and brother sat and listened.

"**Drugs** will destroy you. Drugs **kill**!" said Lilla Belle. "You should never ever use anything that will harm or kill you. Period."

"That's right. Drugs destroy and kill. Nothing good comes from using drugs," said Ben Wongley. "Great answer, Lilla Belle!"

"Zach, should you try drugs even once?" his mother asked.

"No, Mom," said Zach. "Not even once."

"That's correct, Son," said Lea Wongley. "Does it matter what kind of drug it is, Lilla Belle?"

"No, Mother. It doesn't matter what kind of drug it is. If it's not prescribed by a doctor, a licensed physician, I'm not going to take it. Besides," the little girl added, "I love my life and health too much, to risk either. I love being alive and well!" Lilla Belle flashed a winning smile.

****

"Great response, Lilla Belle! I'm proud of both of your answers," said their mother.

"Isn't alcohol a drug?" Zach asked his parents.

"Yes," said Ben Wongley. "Alcohol is a drug. You two are too young to even think about drinking. And while you are under our roof, or I should say, until you become adults, drinking alcohol is definitely off limits." Lilla Belle and Zach nodded. "Zach, should you or your sister, hang around anyone who is a drug user?"

"No, Daddy, we shouldn't," said Zach.

"That is correct," said his father.

"What about us, Lilla Belle?" Lea Wongley asked her daughter. "Should your father and I do drugs, or hang around people who use drugs?"

Lilla Belle shook her head no. "No, Mom. Drugs are very bad; therefore, no one should use them, including you and Daddy. You'll shouldn't hang around people who do drugs either. Grandma Ella says that birds of a feather flock together. As parents, you should **always lead by example,** because as **children**, we **follow your lead**!" Her **parents** looked at each other.

"Are you sure you're only five? I'll have to check your birth certificate," Lea Wongley teased her daughter. Lilla Belle was very wise for her years. "You're absolutely correct, Lilla Belle. You made an excellent point, too. Parents, should always, lead by example. Now, let's talk about **sexual abuse**. What does inappropriate mean, Zach?"

"Something that's not proper. Something that is not right," said Zach.

"That is correct, Son," said his mother.

"Lilla Belle, name the private parts," said her father.

"There are four. The vagina, penis, breasts, and... buttocks. I would also like to add that I know where they are, too, because Mom showed me," said Lilla Belle.

Her parents smiled and nodded. Ben and Lea knew that it was important for their children to know what the private parts were, and where they were located.

"Zach, if anyone touched one of your private areas, what should you do?" his mother asked.

"I would tell you and Dad right away. If I were somewhere else, like school or at Aunt Monica's, I would tell an adult. I would tell someone in authority. But I would always tell you'll, too, as soon as possible." His parents nodded.

"**No one**, be it me, your dad, aunts, uncles, siblings, cousins, pastors, teachers; absolutely no one, **should touch your private areas**. Even if anyone touched you in a way that made you feel uncomfortable, tell them to stop, and let them know that you are going to tell someone in authority. In this case, it is perfectly okay to tell 'anyone' no, and be firm. And **don't ever let anyone persuade you not to tell**. Even if the person threatens you, no matter what they tell you, **always tell**. 'Anyone' who touches your private area(s) is doing something that is very horrible and wrong. No one, should ever do anything like that. I will repeat, telling someone in authority, is **very important**. And, Zach, as you said earlier, make sure that you tell us as soon as possible, too. As your parents, we need to know, and we want to know. **33% of children who are sexually abused are under age six**. The abuser is rarely a stranger. It is almost always a family member or someone that you know, or someone that we know. Sexual abuse is also against the law," said Lea Wongley.

Ben Wongley looked at his children. "It's also important to remember that the person will often try to bribe you with nice things such as toys and money, or they may even offer to buy you whatever you would like. It does not matter what they offer to buy you or how much money they offer to give you. Do not accept anything from them, and don't let anyone stop you from telling an adult, and from telling us. Never worry about whether or not we'll believe you. We are your parents. We will love and support you, no matter what."

"Who does your body belong to, Lilla Belle?" her mother asked.

"Me, Mom. My body belongs to me!" said Lilla Belle.

"That's right, sweetheart," said her mother.

"Mom, Dad, may I please sing a little chant about sexual abuse?" Her parents nodded. Everyone watched as Lilla Belle took the floor. She looked lovingly at her brother. "Okay, Zach. I hope that you and I are never sexually abused, but here is my little chant. Here is what I would do. It's also what I want you, and all children to do... Okay, here goes... I'M GOING TO TELL! I'M GOING TO YELL! SO COPS CAN PUT THAT MONSTER UNDER THE JAIL!" Lilla Belle sang those words again and again. When she took her seat, her family clapped for her.

"That was great, Lilla Belle!" said Zach. "And very creative, too. That is a fantastic chant for all children to remember."

"I second that motion, Lilla Belle!" said her mother, smiling.

"I third the motion!" said her father.

"It's important to remember that abuse is never your fault, so don't ever think that it is or let anyone tell you that it is," said Lea Wongley. "The problem lies with the abuser."

"Mom, Dad? I'd like to make a request."

"What's your request, Lilla Belle?" her mother asked.

"I would like Zach to sing The Lilla Belle Anti-Sexual Abuse Chant. I want to make sure that he has it down pat."

"Lilla Belle!" her brother exclaimed.

"Please, Zach!" said Lilla Belle. "Please!"

"O-kay. Okay. It is kinda cute," said Zach.

"Here's your microphone, Donny," said his sister, handing him an ink pen.

"Thanks, Marie. Okay... here goes. I'm going to tell! I'm going to yell! So cops can put that monster under the jail!" Zach really enjoyed the chant. The words were very easy to remember, too.

"Round of applause for Zach!" said his parents in unison.

"Great job, Donny!" said Lilla Belle, clapping. "Great job!"

"Are we clear on what's been discussed so far?" Ben asked his children. Lilla Belle and Zach nodded. "Good," said their father. "What about child abuse? Say, for instance, you think a child is being abused. What should you do, Zach?"

"I would tell someone in authority. **Child abuse** is very serious, and it can also lead to death," said Zach.

"Yes, Zach, you're right," said his mother. "Not only does physical abuse affect children physically, it can also affect them mentally. Any form of abuse, can shatter a child emotionally, too. You should always tell someone in authority. Anything that is life threatening is worth telling; it's worth acting upon immediately. **It could save a child's life**. Child abuse is also against the law."

"And even if you're wrong, it's better to be safe than sorry," their father added.

"The one word that we can't stress enough. Tell! Always tell. Abused children will often deny that they are being abused, because they're very frightened. They are afraid of what their abuser might do to them if they were to tell someone," said their mother.

"Mommie, Daddy, if I'm being abused in any way, by 'anyone,' I should always tell someone in authority, right?" said Lilla Belle. Her parents nodded. "And children should always tell their parents, too, unless, their parents are the abusers."

"Yes, Lilla Belle, great point! You are correct. And in the event of any **emergency**, always **dial 911**," said her mother.

"Strangers. Should you talk to strangers, Zach?" his father asked.

"No. Never talk to strangers," said Zach.

"Should you go anywhere with anyone that you don't know, Lilla Belle?" asked her mother.

"No. We shouldn't go anywhere with strangers. It's okay to speak to someone if they speak to you, but that is it. That's also optional. If someone whom I don't know wants me to talk to them, I will not, nor should I, talk to them. It wouldn't matter if they tried to lure me with toys, candy, or money. It does not matter; we are never to accept presents, go with strangers, or converse with them."

"That's right, Lilla Belle," said her father.

"Zach, what if a stranger tells you that your father and I sent them to get you and your sister, or just you?" his mother asked.

"We wouldn't go. I would not go. You would never send anyone to pick us up whom we didn't know. And even if we knew the person, you and Dad would always tell us in advance that they were going to pick us up. You would always tell us first. Always!" said Zach.

Lilla Belle waited for her brother to finish. "We should never wander off either! When we're at malls, parks, or any place in general, we should always stay together. We should always stay with you and Daddy," said Lilla Belle. "I've heard many horror stories about children of all ages being taken, seized, and never being seen or heard from again. I don't want that to happen to me or Zach. It doesn't take long for anyone to take a child. I have seen this on *Larry King Live*, so I know that it's true. It's not just hearsay or something to scare kids. It's real!"

"That's right, Lilla Belle. It's all true. It's definitely not hearsay," said her mother. "Zach, you made another excellent point. You're right, your father and I would never send anyone to get either of you, together or individually, without telling you first. **Never go anywhere with strangers**. That is the bottom line."

"What happens if someone does snatch you, Lilla Belle? What should you do then?"

"I would scream bloody murder, Daddy," said Lilla Belle. "I would keep screaming at the top of my lungs, non-stop." Lilla Belle stood up to demonstrate. "Help! Somebody help me! This stranger is taking me! Help! Help me! He-ee-ll-pp!!! I don't know this person! Somebody help me! I don't know this person! I would keep screaming those words over and over again. I would also use my martial arts. I would fight with all of the strength that I have in me!"

Her brother covered his ears. "For such a little person, Lilla Belle, you sure do have a very big voice!"

"You think that's loud, Zach? If anyone grabs me, I would turn up the volume even more," said Lilla Belle. "Under those circumstances, it would behoove me to scream so loudly, that the entire world would be able to hear me. Even the astronauts on the moon would be able to hear me!"

Her mother laughed. "Fantastic, Lilla Belle! You are right, too. Scream bloody murder, sweetheart. And fight!"

"And for kids who don't know martial arts? What could they do, Lilla Belle?" her father asked.

"They could bite, kick, scratch, hit, and/or do any and everything within their power to make the person let them go. Hopefully, the person would let them go, and they or we, would need to run as fast as we could, away from the person who's trying to take us. Run very fast! You don't want to give that person another chance to take you. Get away as quickly as possible and as far away from that person as possible. And it's extremely important to keep screaming, even while you are running. This action will let others know that you're in trouble. It will let them know that something is very wrong. It's also very important to remember, that if I'm running, and the person who is trying to take me, is driving a car, I need to run in the opposite direction. Never run in the same direction that the car is going in. The next important step is running to safety, running to a safe place. For example, running to an area where there are a lot of people, or running into a store. A public place. Run to an adult and tell them what happened. Ask them to call 911 and to call your parents. And, of course, if you spot a police officer or anyone who is in law enforcement, run straight to them and tell them what happened. And, oh, yes, in this case, you may have to talk to a person that you don't know, but don't go anywhere with them either. Hmmm... Did I miss anything?" Lilla Belle asked.

"I don't think so, sweetheart," said her mother.

Lea Wongley was very impressed. Her daughter's memory was sharp and vivid. Lilla Belle was like a sponge, she absorbed everything.

"Zach, what if someone snatched you quickly, then put you into the trunk of a car?" his father asked.

"If I'm in a trunk, it would be hard for anyone to hear me, even if I screamed. In that situation, you showed me and Lilla Belle how to disconnect the taillights, by disconnecting the wires, so I would do that immediately. That should draw attention, especially from law enforcement, and it may even cause an accident. Anyway, once the car stopped for any reason, I would scream, non-stop, at the top of my lungs, and I would keep hitting and kicking the trunk, hoping that someone would hear me."

"Great answer, Zach! You're right," said his mother. "Let's go back to screaming and fighting. If someone is trying to take you, it's very important to remember, that if the person has a weapon, you need to do as you are told. Always proceed with caution. And always stay alert and wait for any opportunity that may come up." The children nodded.

"Now, let's talk about another form of **child abduction**," said Benjamin Wongley. "This kind of abduction happens in the place where one should feel the safest, **at home**. More and more children are being taken from their homes; therefore, it's very important that we discuss this, also. Now, as you both know, every night when your mother and I tuck you in, we check your windows to make sure that they are completely closed and locked. The pins that we've shown both of you are also added security. This makes it more difficult for someone trying to enter in through the windows."

"Along with the wind chimes, too. Right, Dad?" Zach asked. "I mean for added security, to alert us."

"You're exactly right, Son," said his father. "Wind chimes were purposely placed by your windows, so that it makes it easier for you to hear someone if they are trying to enter in through your windows. We also make sure that your curtains are closed. **Never**, ever, **unlock** the **windows** or open the curtains after we've closed and locked them. The windows are closed and locked for your safety and protection. We close the curtains for the same reason. We don't want anyone looking in, seeing you, and seeing where you are. We don't want anyone coming in through the window, taking you away from us, and even worse, killing you. Is this clear?" The children nodded. "However, if either of you ever hear noises outside your windows, or see shadows, I want you to run and get us right away. Do not go to the window, and don't try to do any investigating. And by all means, please don't ignore it. Again, come and get us right away. Am I making myself perfectly clear?"

"Yes, Daddy," said Lilla Belle and Zach in unison.

"If you are wrong, that's perfectly okay, too," said their mother. "And to take it further, if someone is breaking in and they are coming through your bedroom window, or any window or door for that matter, run as fast as you can out of the room and scream at the top of your lungs to get our attention. But remember, safety comes first, so get out of the room, get out of harm's way quickly. Don't wait around or linger. And never, ever, try to play the hero. Now, if someone does break in, and you are unable to get away from them, if, for example, they tell you to keep quiet, do as you're told, if they have a weapon. But try to knock something over, such as a lamp perhaps, anything, to make noise." The children nodded.

"And, as we have told you before, always **look** through the peephole **BEFORE unlocking** the **door**," said Ben Wongley. "And if ever in doubt, never open the door. We can never say what will or won't happen. But we can prepare you and try to prevent anything horrible from happening. And if someone does try to break in the house, we certainly don't want to make it easy for them. At the very least, if doors and windows are locked, we'll be able to hear them if they are trying to break in. You can have all of the money in the world, you can live in the best neighborhood, however, no one, is excluded from crime or tragedy. No one! We all live in the same world." The children sat listening. "We have a top-notch security system; therefore, it should go off if anyone ever does try to break in, but alarms can break down like anything else. We have motion detectors, too, which are also very helpful. But the most important thing, the bottom line, is to prepare you," Ben told his children.

"Again, use what you know," said their mother. "And take what we teach you, wherever you go. According to statistics, **76% of children are taken by family members or someone they know. 24% of kidnapped children are taken by strangers. And 85-90% of missing children are under eighteen**. Both of you are too young to have a grasp about percentages, but just know that those numbers prove, that the majority of children are taken by relatives and by people whom children actually know. Any questions?" Lilla Belle and Zach shook their heads no. "What is **peer pressure**, Zach?" his mother asked.

"Being pressured by your friends to do something. It's usually what a lot of people are doing, so it's usually popular," Zach replied.

"That's right, Son," said Lea Wongley. "What do you think about peer pressure, Lilla Belle?"

"Even though I've just started school?" Her mother nodded. "Well, if peer pressure means being pressured to do something by your peers, it would depend on whether or not it was right or wrong. And that goes back to morals, values, and integrity. If I pressured my best friend, Ivana, to do anything, I'm not being a good friend. Ask or give advice in some cases, but do not pressure. **True friends will always want what is best for you.** I also know that you don't just do anything simply because other people are doing it, especially, if it's wrong. As Grandma Ella says, be your own person, and use your own head! She says that God gave us our very own heads for a reason. My head is for me to use! I will always use my own head," Lilla Belle said wisely.

"That's right, Lilla Belle," said her mother.

"You and Daddy are our parents, and you'll love me and Zach to pieces. You both want what is best for us. That is why we have these meetings!"

"You're right again, Lilla Belle," said her father. "We love you'll to smithereens!"

"We love you'll very much," said Lea Wongley. "Now, getting back to the subject at hand, **what is popular isn't always right**, and what's right, isn't always popular. **Doing what's right, is** very **important**. **Even if you stand alone**, and even if you're outnumbered. Just know that when you do what's right, you are in an elite group. Many people can follow, but not everyone can lead."

"**Smoking**. Is it okay to smoke, Zach?" Ben asked his son.

"No, Daddy, it isn't. Smoking is bad for you. It is very **harmful to** your **health**. It can cause lung disease and cancer," said Zach.

"Right, Zach! We have all seen the ads. We've all heard the 'smoking is cool' slogan. **There is absolutely nothing cool about anything, that's bad for you**, be it: drugs, skipping school, drinking alcohol, smoking, using bad words, breaking rules, the list is long. So **many things are labeled as 'cool**,' but it's very important to remember, **what's really cool**, **is always**, **that which is right, good for you, and healthy**. Never forget that," Ben told his children.

"Your father is right. That's why it is very **important to surround yourself with people who are mirrors of you**. When I say mirrors of you, I don't mean people who look like you, I mean **people who 'are' like you**. People with the same morals and the same values. People with integrity. People who want the very best for themselves and want the best out of life," Lea Wongley explained.

"Do either of you have anything that you would like to say?" Ben asked his children.

"No, Daddy," said Zach.

"I love these meetings!" said Lilla Belle. "I feel so very powerful. I feel like a Powerpuff Girl! These meetings remind me of school. In a way, it is like school because we're being taught about things that are very important. I feel a whole lot better knowing about these things, rather than not knowing. Not knowing, would scare me," said Lilla Belle. "I've got the power to devour the bad guy!"

Her mother laughed. "We discussed a variety of topics today. Is there 'anything,' that you didn't completely understand?"

"No, Mommie," said Lilla Belle.

"I don't have any questions, Mom," Zach replied.

"It's important to us that we teach you and have an honest and open relationship with you. We are your **parents**. **Teaching starts at home**. And by us. We want you to always remember, that there's not a certain time or day that you can talk to us. Come to us anytime," their mother said.

"About anything," said their father.

Ben and Lea Wongley knew that **good information** was the **best friend of prevention**. Not only had they always supplied their children with unconditional love and parental guidance, but they also knew how important it was to **arm** their **children with knowledge**. The Wongleys knew that knowledge was power, and sharing it was empowerment. They were determined to keep their children empowered. As far as they were concerned, being a good parent wasn't an option. It was a necessity.

Lea Wongley looked at her children and smiled. She loved them so much. And she wanted the very best for them. She and Ben were going to do everything within their power, to ensure that their children grew up to be happy, healthy, intelligent, and confident individuals, with great morals, values, and integrity.

"Great job you two!" said Ben and Lea Wongley in unison.

"There was one important topic that we didn't discuss," said Lilla Belle.

"Oh?" said her mother.

"A raise for my allowance," Lilla Belle quipped. "Zach's, too."

"Nice try, pretty girl!" Everyone laughed. "Your father and I will think about it. Now, on a more serious note, as **parents**, we **are not just** your **first teachers**," said their mother.

"We are **also** your **most important teachers**," their father finished.

The Wongleys ended the conference with their usual group hug.

*Chapter Four*
**The Bully Giants**

As time went on, Lilla Belle and Ivana met other students in their school. They'd heard a lot about "the bully giants." The bully giants were two third graders, who were taller and much larger than their classmates. They were known for bullying the smaller children.

One day, while Lilla Belle, Ivana, Mara, and some other girls, whom the kindergartners didn't know, were in the rest room washing their hands after recess, the bully giants walked in.

"Uh-oh," Mara said to Lilla Belle and Ivana. "We'd better go now."

"You'll ain't goin' nowhere!" said June, the larger bully giant. Her eyes were like green ice, as she looked down at Mara.

"You all will go when we tell you'll to go," said Rose, the other bully giant. "We runnin' thangs! Tha po' people runnin' thangs today." Rose looked at Lilla Belle with cold gray eyes. "Lilla Belle! Lilla Belle! I hear bells of money rangin'. Rich girl! Moneybags! I'm tired of ridin' aroun' in my Mom's ol' green car, seein' Wongley this and Wongley that, all aroun' town. We ain't got tha kinda dough you have, Miss southern belle! My, you so pretty! You real pretty, Miss Lilla Belle!"

"Ain't she though? She's as pretty as can be! Everybody ain't able! It must be nice to be so pretty. And rich!" said June, with a smirk on her face. June tossed her long blonde hair. "Tha Wongley name's on everythang! And you ride aroun' in that rich man's car. That gorgeous red BMW! Everybody ain't able to do what tha Wongleys do. Huh, Rose?"

"And you know this," said Rose.

"Rose, what do you think BMW stands fo'?"

"Hmmm... How 'bout, BIG, MONEY, Wongley?!" said Rose. Both bully giants laughed.

"You and yo' family's nothin' but show offs! And you, Ivana, don't think we gonna leave you out. You live in tha rich part of Beaver Creek, too," said June. "Right down tha street from this other Miss Richie-rich. Yo' momma thinks she so pretty drivin' that black convertible Jag. I neva see her wit' tha top down. What's wrong wit' her? Afraid she gone get her hair messed up?"

"Now, June, why you talkin' 'bout that girl's momma like that? You know you wrong fo' that!" Rose laughed. "Shemara! Miss Washington! You live fo' blocks away from these two, so that means you ain't doin' too bad neither!"

"I ain't seen yo' folks yet. What do you drive?" June asked, eyeing Mara.

"A black car," Mara whispered.

The bully giant stood, looking at Mara, angrily. "Ha! Ha! Ha! Tryin' to be smart, huh? I didn't find that funny!" yelled June. "A bit of advice for ya. Don't quit ya day job, sweetie! That wasn't what I meant, and you know it!" The bully giant continued. "I 'said' what yo' car called? Tha name. What is tha 'name' of yo' car?" June insisted.

"Answer, little ol' girl!" said Rose.

"I don't have a car. I'm too young to drive," said Mara, who was scared stiff.

"You know, for someone who don't even weigh five pounds soakin' wet, you sho' got a smart mouth on ya. You light as a feather. I can blow you away with one breath. Big money Washington's a smart aleck, ain't she, Rose? Let's give her one good beatin', so she know next time not to get smart wit' us! Let's sho' her what time it is. Somebody shoulda told her we ain't tha ones!"

June swung at Mara. Lilla Belle blocked her swing and held her arm in a wrist claw, a jujitsu technique that she learned from Master Ching in martial arts class.

"Ouch! Ouch! Let me go! Rose! DO somethin'!" Rose swung at Lilla Belle. Lilla Belle blocked her swing, too, while still holding June's arm in a wrist claw. Ivana and Mara grabbed both bully giants by their waists. They didn't have to do anything though. It was very obvious that Lilla Belle could easily hold her own.

"I'm not releasing neither of you until you'll promise to leave us alone. We don't bother you, and you're not going to bother us either. Don't bother us again, ever," said Lilla Belle, firmly. She looked the bully giants in the eye to let them know she meant business.

"Okay!" the bully giants yelled. "Okay! We promise! Please! Please! Let us go!" June and Rose begged Lilla Belle. "Please!"

Lilla Belle released them. The bully giants ran out of the rest room, in great pain, and very embarrassed.

The other girls in the rest room looked on in shock. How could tiny Lilla Belle take on the bully giants so easily? They all wondered. She made it look so easy!

"I was scared! But we were going to go down together," said Ivana.

"That's right!" said Lilla Belle.

"That sure is right!" said Mara. "Ivana, we didn't have to grab either of them. Wow, Lilla Belle! You are one tough cookie. How...? How did you do that? Those girls are HUGE!"

"Yeah, real BIG!" Ivana said, agreeing with Mara.

Lilla Belle looked at both of her friends. "Ladies, it's not the size of the girl in the fight, it's the size of the fight in the girl."

"Grandma Ella again?" Ivana asked.

"That is correct, Wise-one," said Lilla Belle, quoting Master Ching.

As the three girls entered the hallway, Ivana turned towards Lilla Belle. "I want to learn what you know. It can certainly come in handy."

Lilla Belle smiled and shook her head. "I can't tell."

"Why not?" Ivana asked.

"Ancient Japanese secret," Lilla Belle whispered.

"Huh?" said Mara.

"I was just kidding," said Lilla Belle. "Mother, Zach, and I go to martial arts class four days a week. We learn self-defense. We also learn discipline, self-respect, and self-esteem. Correction, Zach and I are taught those things by Mom and Dad. In regard to self-defense, we learn, study, and practice, each time that we go to martial arts class. If you think I'm good, you should see Daddy, Zach, and Uncle Jesse! Mommie can hold her own, too!"

"Apparently, so can you!" said Ivana. Mara nodded her head in agreement. "You were really awesome, Lilla Belle."

"You go, girl!" said Mara, smiling.

"Can we go to martial arts class with you from now on?" Ivana asked Lilla Belle.

"I will have to ask my mother, and you two will have to ask your parents," said Lilla Belle.

****

News of what had taken place spread quickly throughout the school. When Zach heard about what happened, he checked on his sister to make sure that she was okay.

"I figured you were," said Zach, sounding relieved. "Now that I know you're okay, I'm okay. See you later!" Zach hurried to his class before the bell rang.

****

"Lilla Belle, I've never seen Shemara's parents. Have you?" Ivana asked Lilla Belle, during the ride home that day.

"No, I've never seen Mara's parents either."

"Ah-ha! You're calling her Mara, too, just like her aunt and the rest of the class," Ivana said.

"Yes, I sure am. You're late, Ivana, I've been calling her Mara for two whole days now," said Lilla Belle. "How do you know her aunt calls her 'Mara'?"

"Because! She told all of us when she introduced herself on the first day of school. Remember?" said Ivana.

"That's right. I had forgotten. She sure did. It's all coming back to me now!" Lilla Belle sang.

"YOU forgot? Lilla Belle, are you okay? It's not like you to forget anything!" Both girls laughed.

That night, at dinner, Zach teased his sister. "Pass me the rolls, please, Lilla Belle Lee," said Zach.

"Lilla Belle Lee?" asked their mother.

"Mom, Dad, I had a fight today in school. If you want to call it that," said Lilla Belle.

"A fight? Sweetheart, what happened?" her mother asked.

"Me, Ivana, and Mara, another kindergartner, were in the rest room, and these two big homely girls came in and started teasing us for being rich. When they asked Mara what kind of car she drove, they didn't like her answer, so they swung at her, and I stopped them from hitting Mara. I like her, Mom and Dad, she's really nice. Ivana likes her, too. Anyway, that's basically it," said Lilla Belle.

"Those girls were big, too!" said Zach. "Think David and Goliath. But Miss Lee handled them like paper dolls. They won't bother my little sister again. Way to go, Lilla Belle Lee!"

"Lilla Belle, how big were these girls?" her father asked.

"They were big, almost as big as you and Mommie, but I wasn't afraid. I took care of things. I know that you don't encourage Zach and me to fight, but in that case, I didn't have a choice." Her parents nodded.

"Call me at work if you need to, Lilla Belle," said her father.

"I will be at home all day tomorrow, sweetheart," said her mother. "You know our cell phone numbers, too." Lilla Belle smiled and nodded.

"And I will be at school tomorrow, Miss Lee, should you need me." Zach laughed. "But, something tells me that you won't!"

The next morning, all of the girls who were in the rest room during the time of the incident were called to the principal's office for questioning.

"Called for questioning? Are we going to jail?" Mara asked. She had a very serious look on her face. Her two friends laughed.

"I seriously doubt it," said Lilla Belle. "But, girls, if we do get locked up, I know that we are allowed at least one phone call."

"Who would you call, Lilla Belle, your parents?" Ivana asked. "Or Grandma Ella?"

Lilla Belle shook her head no. "Johnnie Cochran." Mara looked frightened. "Relax, Miss Washington, I'm just kidding! We're off to see Mr. Stavros. Stavros. I like that last name. It's different. I've seen the principal before. He reminds me of Richard Roundtree! How cool is that?" said Lilla Belle.

"Who's Richard Roundtree?" Ivana asked.

"The actor who played in several movies with Julia Roberts," Mara said.

"Nooo...!" said Lilla Belle, laughing. "That was Richard Gere! Richard Roundtree is the actor who starred in the original Shaft." Lilla Belle was still giggling about Mara's answer when they approached the principal's office.

All of the girls who witnessed the incident told the principal that Lilla Belle simply defended herself and stopped the bully giants from hitting Mara.

"It wasn't Lilla Belle's fault. She's innocent. Although Lilla Belle certainly could've hurt the bully giants, she didn't hurt them, Mr. Stavros," said a tall thin girl with short red hair and freckles. "It was the bully giants' fault. They started it!"

Lilla Belle had seen her in the hallway many times, but she didn't know the girl's name.

"The bully giants?" Mr. Stavros asked, looking puzzled. "Who are the bully giants?" he asked again, still waiting for an answer. Mara pointed at Rose and June. "I see..." said Mr. Stavros, nodding. The principal told Rose and June to apologize to Lilla Belle, Mara, and Ivana.

"We're sorry," they mumbled.

Mr. Stavros told everyone to go back to class. "Rose and June? I need to speak with both of you," said the principal. "Close the door behind you, please. Have a seat." When Rose and June took their seats, Mr. Stavros continued. "If either of you would have hit Mara, or any student for that matter, you would have been expelled from school. We neither support nor tolerate violence of any kind here at Jones. Zero tolerance! All of my students will come to this school with peace of mind. Is this understood? Am I making myself clear?" Mr. Stavros paused, as he looked at Rose and June, waiting for an answer.

"Yes, suh," June replied.

"I understand," said Rose.

"This incident will be recorded in each of your files. I'm also going to call your parents." The principal buzzed his secretary. "Mrs. Riegel?"

"Yes, Mr. Stavros?" Mrs. Riegel replied.

"Please bring me the phone numbers of June Walker's and Rose Bruce's parents." The principal turned his attention back to Rose and June. "I don't want to see or hear of you two threatening or inflicting violence on anyone, student or teacher, ever. Once again, do I make myself perfectly clear?"

"Yes, suh, Mr. Stavros," said June.

"Yes, suh," Rose said.

"Good," said the principal. "It's very important to respect yourself and to respect others. It's also important to treat people the way that you yourself would like to be treated. Both of you may have heard this before, but I will reiterate it. Violence is NOT the answer, nor will it be tolerated here at Jones. Do either of you have anything that you would like to say?" Mr. Stavros asked.

"No, suh," said the bully giants in unison.

"Okay, you both need to see Mrs. Riegel on your way out. She will have your detention information."

The girls nodded as they walked to the secretary's office.

*Chapter Five*
**Shemara**

The days were hot and humid. Most of the children at school wore shorts. As long as they were knee length and not cut-offs, shorts were okay to wear to school.

Lilla Belle thought it strange that Mara never wore shorts. Even more unusual was the fact that, as hot as it was, Mara always wore long-sleeved shirts, too. I'm going to ask Mara, Lilla Belle thought. Then again, Lilla Belle continued to think, Mara could be cold-natured like her aunt.

Aunt Shevette kept the heater on at her home in Bryan, even during the summer. Uncle Jesse would look at her in disbelief, often shaking his head. Lilla Belle still loved going over to her aunt's house. Aunt Shevette was one of her favorite aunts.

During recess that day, as Lilla Belle, Ivana, and Mara were walking on the playground, Lilla Belle asked her friend the question she had been pondering.

"It's not hot to me," Mara told Lilla Belle and Ivana, as she looked down towards the ground. "Hey, let's see who can make it to the swings first!" said Mara. Lilla Belle and Ivana raced Mara to the swings. “I won!” Mara shouted.

“You should’ve won,” said Ivana. “You had a head start, Mara.”

Mara had incredible speed. Lilla Belle and Ivana both knew that Mara would have won without a head start. She was very fast!

The girls always looked forward to recess. This, for them, was fun time. They also got plenty of exercise in the process.

****

Mara was usually the last kindergartner to get picked up from school. Her father, Michael Washington, was an attorney. He had his own law firm.

Many times, especially if Mara’s father was in court, he would be running a little late picking his daughter up.

Mara and Miss Monner would often talk about school while waiting for her father to arrive.

“You can leave, Miss Monner,” said Mara. “I can wait outside for my dad.”

“Oh, no, young lady. I’m going to wait here with you. I wouldn’t even think of doing such a thing!” Minutes later, Miss Monner spotted the black BMW. “Mara, speaking of your father, he’s pulling up now. Do you have all of your things?”

“Yes, ma’am,” said Mara.

“How is my little pumpkin?” Michael Washington asked his daughter, minutes later, as he gave her a hug.

“I’m fine, Daddy,” Mara answered.

“Thanks for waiting with her, Miss Monner. I am so sorry that I’m late again,” said Mara’s father.

“That’s okay, Mr. Washington. You were only fifteen minutes late,” said Miss Monner, looking at the clock.

"How is Mara doing in school?" Michael Washington asked the teacher.

"Mara is doing excellent! She is very smart. She already knew how to write her name, how to count to one hundred, and she also knew the alphabet, from day one," said Miss Monner. "Mara is very well-behaved, too."

"Aunt Bee taught me a lot!" said Mara, smiling.

"Your aunt taught you very well," said the teacher.

"I'm glad to hear that," said Michael Washington. "Ready to go, Mara?"

"Yes, Daddy. 'Bye, Miss Monner!" said Mara.

"Good-bye, Mara, see you tomorrow."

****

The Washingtons lived two blocks from the school and four blocks from Mara's two best friends, Lilla Belle and Ivana.

Michael Washington parked in front of his townhouse. "No, I'll go ahead and park in the garage," he said. "Looks like it's going to rain."

Shortly after arriving home, Michael checked his voice mail. "Yes! She called! Natalie called!" said Mike, who was thrilled beyond words.

This call had made Mike's day. He didn't think this lady would ever call him back. He had actually given up on her. Natalie was a lady Mike had met two weeks ago. He had asked her out on a date, and they had exchanged phone numbers, but until now, she had never returned his calls.

Mara did her homework and wrote a letter to her Aunt Bee, whose real name was Annie Jackson, but everyone who knew her, called her "Aunt Bee."

Mara had given many letters to her father to mail for her, but her aunt never wrote back. Mara also wondered why her aunt never called or visited her. Maybe Aunt Bee's too sick to call, write, or visit, thought Mara.

In reality, Mara's father never mailed the letters. He would take the letters that his daughter gave him and throw them away.

Aunt Bee called many times, only to be threatened by Mike, who told her that if she didn't stop calling, he would have his phone number changed and unpublished.

Mara's aunt continued to call. She pleaded with Mike to let her speak with her niece.

"No!" Michael Washington would often yell. "Stay out of our lives! This is the last time you will call my home and harass us!"

Aunt Bee didn't have their address either. Michael Washington made sure of that. He used his knowledge of the law, and his resources, to ensure that Aunt Bee stayed out of their lives.

"You're not going to poison my daughter against me," he'd told her the last time they had spoken on the phone. "Shemara's older now. I'm not going to have her hating me."

Aunt Bee spent her entire life savings fighting Michael Washington in court, but the law was clearly on his side. He was Mara's natural father, and Michael and Denise, Mara's mother, were married and living together at the time of her death.

Michael Washington fought to make sure that Mara had his last name, too. Aunt Bee had originally given Mara her last name.

"You're fortunate that I'm even allowing her to live with you. I can take my daughter at any time, you know. Keep that in mind, Annie," he'd told her one day in court.

Aunt Bee had always hoped and prayed that day would never come, but when Mara turned five years old, the trouble began...

Mara had lived with her aunt since birth. Aunt Bee was her great aunt, she was her grandmother's sister.

Mara's mother died shortly after giving birth to her. Denise had been rushed to the hospital by ambulance, badly beaten and near death. She'd almost had a miscarriage.

Aunt Bee had Michael Washington arrested. He had beaten Denise many times before. Aunt Bee begged and pleaded with her niece to leave him. Denise would leave sometimes, but she would always go back to her husband.

"Aunt Bee..." Denise spoke slowly.

It pained Aunt Bee greatly to see her niece, lying in the hospital bed, badly beaten and in so much pain.

"Denise, please, please don't try to speak now. Save your strength," said Aunt Bee.

"No..." said Denise. "Please, lis-ten... lis-ten... to me."

"We can talk when you're well again," Aunt Bee told her, trying to sound encouraging.

But Denise went on, "I've had too man-y, too man-y, beat-ings, too man-y... I, I..." She looked almost lifeless.

Aunt Bee held Denise's hand and said a silent prayer for her. "Denise..." Aunt Bee could see that it was very difficult for Denise to speak. She also knew, all too well, how stubborn her niece could be.

"I... want... you... please... name her, She-mar-a... She-mar-a. My baby's name... She-mar-a. I've always... I've al-ways liked that name. Tell her, tell... my baby, tell my little girl... Mom-mie... will... al-ways love her. Love her, teach her... Aunt Bee. I don't want her to end up like me. Don't let her make the same mis-takes that I've made. Please... do that for me, Aunt Bee..."

"Oh, Denise..." said a tearful Aunt Bee.

Denise looked at her aunt. Her dark eyes were filled with tears and regret. "I, I... should've lis-tened... to you and Aunt Reen. Tell her not to let... any, any man, any per-son, beat... her. Pray, that the man who... finds her, one day, will be good to her... for... her, be very good to She-mar-a, my... ba-by. I've made so many mis-takes. My, my...one regret is... that I... I won't live to see my ba-by... grow up." Tears rolled down Denise's face. Aunt Bee couldn't refrain from crying either. Denise managed a slight smile. Her once beautiful face was barely recognizable. "Aunt Bee... you know... I have nev-er liked the word good-bye... Thank... you for tak-ing me in... Thanks for tak-ing care of me... for lov-ing me. You were always, al-ways there for me... I love you very much, Aunt Bee. Prom-ise me, that you... will take care of her, my... my ba-by. Please, please, don't... let... Mi, She...mar-a..." Denise never finished her sentence. Her eyes closed. It appeared that she had stopped breathing.

"Denise! Denise!" Aunt Bee cried, shaking her. "Oh, God! Doctor! Doctor!" Aunt Bee cried frantically.

"Ms. Jackson, please go to the waiting room," said Dr. Wagner. "Please, Ms. Jackson."

The doctor came out to the waiting room a short time later. "I'm sorry, Ms. Jackson. We did all we could do. I am... so sorry."

"Oh, God!" cried Aunt Bee, hugging her best

friend. “Corine! Corine! My baby! Oh, God!”

“I’m so sorry, Annie,” Corine told her friend. “I’m... so sorry.”

“Oh, God! Oh, God!” Aunt Bee cried uncontrollably.

“I know,” said Corine, giving her a hug. “Come with me, Annie.”

Aunt Bee and Corine went to the chapel that was located inside of the hospital. They sat in the chapel for hours, crying and talking. Corine wished there was something she could do to take the pain away. All she could do was be there for her friend. She knew Annie needed her more than ever now.

The two women had been best friends for many years. They had always been there for each other.

“I’m here for you, Annie, but more importantly,” said Corine, looking at the cross on the wall, “God’s with you. He is with us, always.”

Corine cried as they sat in the chapel. She had known Denise since birth. She was so full of life, so polite, gorgeous... Corine thought quietly to herself as she remembered Denise.

Denise’s mother, Erica, died in a car accident when Denise was eight years old. Aunt Bee had taken her niece in and raised her. She couldn’t have loved Denise more if she’d been her own daughter.

Corine sat, thinking of Michael Washington with disgust! From the moment Annie and Corine had first met him, neither of them liked him. It was something about that smooth talker. It wasn’t long before they found out why they didn’t like Michael.

Michael Washington was very abusive and controlling. He began physically and verbally abusing Denise before marriage, when they had first started dating.

Annie and Corine pleaded with Denise to leave Mike alone for good, before she ended up dead, or disabled.

"I love him!" Denise would always say. "He loves me, too. Mike will change. He promised me that he wouldn't hit me again. He said he was sorry," she would always tell them, time and time again. Denise always made excuses for Michael Washington. "Look, he bought me this diamond bracelet," she'd told them one day.

"Oh, Denise," Corine said, looking at her shaking her head, "all of the diamonds in the world aren't worth your life! Material things are always replaceable, but your life isn't."

"You know," Aunt Bee went on, "I am going to say exactly what's on my mind. Denise, if you're not careful, he's going to love you to death." Apparently, that is exactly what happened.

Corine looked over at her best friend, who was sitting beside her now, tears steadily streaming down her face.

"I told Denise... I told her! We told her... Oh... my, God! Corine, why didn't, why didn't Denise listen? Why?" cried Aunt Bee. "Why didn't she... Denise was always talking about how much she loved that BEAST!" Aunt Bee sat, shaking her head. "Why didn't she realize how much she should have loved herself? Loving herself enough not to put up with any kind of abuse or mistreatment from ANYONE! Physically, verbally, mentally, emotionally... These are trying times. Oh, God! First, Erica, and now, Denise. God... help me, help us..."

"And He will, Annie, He will help us," said Corine. "He has always helped us."

Corine's heart was very heavy, too. There lay a precious, new born baby girl, who would never know her mother. There lay a young woman, once so full of life, now dead.

Denise was only twenty-three years old. A life abruptly cut short by her very own husband.

Michael Washington walked away scot-free, and more importantly than that, he still had his life. He was not the person lying in a coffin. Denise was.

All of these thoughts ran through Aunt Bee's mind as she sat, thinking about what was before her now. "Self-love is so very important. It's not selfish to love yourself. It's a MUST! Many things start with SELF... Dear, God! Why couldn't we get through to her? Why didn't Denise listen? Why didn't she..." Aunt Bee couldn't stop crying.

****

Aunt Bee named the baby, Shemara Denise. The little girl weighed three pounds. She stayed in the hospital for two weeks.

As time went on, Aunt Bee watched Shemara grow. And how her little niece grew! If only her mother could see her now, Aunt Bee thought to herself, sadly.

Shemara was the spitting image of her mother. She was definitely her mother's daughter.

Aunt Bee began calling her little niece "Mara" shortly after bringing her home from the hospital.

Every year on April 7th, Mara's birthday, Aunt Bee and Corine would throw her a big birthday party. Many of the neighborhood kids would come to Mara's party. This was also a sad day of remembrance. It was the same day that Mara's mother had died.

Aunt Bee remembered that day, years ago, so clearly... Michael Washington was never charged with murder. He had beaten Denise so badly that day.

Denise pleaded with her husband to stop. “Please, Mike, the baby!” Denise cried. “Don’t kill our baby! Mike! Please!” she begged him. Her husband finally left, after beating her to within an inch of her life. She had to save the baby! Denise crawled to the phone and dialed 911.

The police came immediately and found a badly beaten Denise, lying at the bottom of the living room stairs.

“Who did this to you?” the police officers asked her repeatedly, after dispatching the ambulance.

“Please... get me... to the hos...pital,” said Denise, not answering the officers’ question.

“Where is your husband, Mrs. Washington?” Officer Banks asked her. Denise was no longer conscious.

Officer Banks looked in Denise’s wallet to find her emergency contact numbers. The police officers tried unsuccessfully to reach Michael Washington. They left an urgent message on his voice mail.

“His cell phone is either off, or he’s just not answering,” Officer Lloyd told his partner.

Both of the officers believed, that this was another horrible case of domestic violence.

Officer Banks phoned Denise’s aunt, Annie Jackson, who was listed as her next of kin.

“Oh, Lord! God, no! I’m on my way!” Aunt Bee told the police that Michael Washington was responsible. She also told them where they could find him.

Michael Washington was taken into custody, but he was released shortly thereafter. No charges were filed.

"Insufficient evidence," Officer Banks told Aunt Bee. "Mrs. Washington refuses to tell us who did this to her."

There were no prior records of violence either. Denise had never reported her husband. She refused to tell the officers that her husband was responsible for abusing her. She didn't want him to go to jail. Denise loved her husband very much. She was also very fearful of him. Denise always hoped that one day Michael would stop beating her.

Officer Banks never understood why most abused women refused to report their husbands or significant others. He knew fear had a lot to do with it. Many of them would die first, and many often did, without breathing a word to anyone, especially to police. The abused were usually loyal to their abusers.

After leaving the hospital, Officer Banks sat in his car, very angry. He was certain that Michael Washington should be locked up and on his way to prison, but he hadn't even received a slap on the wrist.

And it was all because Mrs. Washington refused to tell them that Michael was responsible for abusing her; she had refused to press charges, even though he almost killed her and their baby.

Officer Banks placed his face in his hands. His heart went out to the aunt, and even more so to the beautiful little girl who would grow up without her mother. Officer Banks doubted very seriously if Denise would live. He had seen her at the hospital. She was hanging on by a thread.

Officer Banks shook his head. He could only imagine how it would feel being a child and knowing that your mother died at the hands of your own father. He couldn't even fathom that. He was also angry because he knew that a monster like Michael Washington would automatically have custody of Shemara.

Officer Banks prayed and hoped that Michael Washington would let the child's aunt raise her. How could he look at that child, knowing what he had done to her mother? How could he?

****

Michael Washington allowed his daughter to live with Aunt Bee, with the previsions that he be able to pick her up and visit her sometimes.

Mike would usually come see Mara every week. He would often bring her expensive gifts, too. The sight of Mike Washington made Aunt Bee's stomach turn. She loathed him!

"Can you buy her mother's life back?" Aunt Bee often asked him. Michael Washington would never answer that question. "All of the fancy gifts and all of the money in the world won't bring her mother back!"

Aunt Bee would only discuss Denise when Mara was out of earshot. She didn't want Mara to hear her. Aunt Bee hadn't told Mara how her mother died. She vowed to protect Mara for as long as she could, especially from that monster. And she had promised her mother as much.

Aunt Bee loved her little niece more than anyone in the world. The two were very close. She was always amused by little Mara's energy, too.

Looking at Mara was like looking at Denise when she was Mara's age. Mara looked more and more like her mother every day.

Aunt Bee was a firm believer in having fun, but she was also a firm believer in teaching and nurturing children. With Mara, she did both. She taught her how to count, how to say her grace and prayers, and how to be polite. “Good manners are important,” Aunt Bee told Mara. She wanted the very best for her little niece. She also told Mara to be the best in her class when she went to school. “Always be the best, Mara. Always!”

****

One summer afternoon, a now five-year-old Mara, went to spend the day with her father.

Her father told her that he was going to take her shopping for school clothes.

“How would you like to stay with Daddy?” Mike Washington asked his daughter.

“Stay? You mean spend the night?” Mara asked.

“No, I mean, how would you like to live with me, permanently, for good?” said her father.

“Can Aunt Bee live with us, too?” asked Mara.

“No, just the two of us. How about it, Mara?”

“No, I want to stay with Aunt Bee!” Mara said.

“Shemara, the truth is, you’ll be staying with me for a while. Aunt Bee’s going into the hospital to have surgery,” her father lied.

“But why didn’t she tell me?” Mara asked.

“She didn’t want you to worry, honey. Don’t look so sad, sweetheart! Look on the bright side of things, this gives us time to spend together. We’ll have a lot of fun! You’ll see.”

“When am I going back to Aunt Bee’s?” Mara asked her father.

"I don't know, Shemara, it all depends on how long it takes your aunt to heal," said Mike.

"We can still go visit her at the hospital. Right, Daddy?" Mara asked.

"Maybe. I've talked to the doctors, and they told me it would be a while before your aunt's able to have visitors. The doctors have my phone number. I will be talking to them every day to see how Aunt Bee's doing. We'll also send flowers and cards to the hospital."

Mara nodded sadly in answer.

****

It was getting later and later. Aunt Bee paced around in her living room. She looked out the window, again and again. Where was Mara? She didn't have a good feeling. She knew something was wrong! She was about to call the police when the phone rang.

"Hello," said Aunt Bee, picking the phone up on the first ring. It was Michael Washington. Aunt Bee recognized the sickening voice all too well.

"Hi. I won't be on the phone long. I've decided to keep my daughter. I have already taken the necessary precautions, should you try anything. The police have already been called, so please don't call them saying I kidnapped her. She's my daughter. I'm the one with legal custody," Mike told her, sounding smug.

Aunt Bee's heart sank. "Where is Mara? Where is my baby?" she asked.

"Thanks for nothing!" said Mike, slamming down the phone.

Devastated, Aunt Bee sat on the sofa. She immediately called her best friend.

"Corine, come over. I need to talk with you."

"I'm coming, Annie. I'll be right over," Corine told her. Corine could hear in her friend's voice that something was terribly wrong.

While driving over to Annie's, she couldn't help but wonder, what did Michael Washington do this time? He was such a cruel, heartless animal.

Corine had always told Annie, that what goes around, comes around, and when Mike's turn came around, he was going to pay dearly! They may or may not be alive to see that day, she'd told Annie, but that dog's day, was definitely going to come.

Upon entering her best friend's home, Aunt Bee immediately told Corine what happened.

"Annie, I knew it! You did, too. That low life scumbag! I can't stand that poor excuse of a man."

"Neither can I, Corine, neither can I." Aunt Bee began breathing hard and heavy.

"Annie! Take it easy! Let me get you something. Have you taken your medicine?"

"Yes, I took my medicine earlier," said Aunt Bee.

"Here, drink this. It's a cold glass of water. You have to relax. Relax, Annie! You're not going to do Mara any good if you get sick," Corine told her, trying to console her best friend, all the while feeling devastated herself.

"Corine, what am I going to do?"

"Annie, there's nothing we can do. The laws are so screwed up these days, it's pathetic! I sometimes think they are designed to protect the creeps who do wrong, instead of the innocent people who do right."

"Amen to that," said Aunt Bee.

"All we can do is pray, Annie. Like all things, it's in God's hands."

As days turned into weeks, and weeks turned into months, Aunt Bee's health began to fail. Corine knew the situation with her little niece was the reason.

It was obvious that Aunt Bee had not been the same since Mara was taken by her father.

Aunt Bee's doctor tried to console her with medicine and advice, but nothing he said or did seemed to do any good.

"Take this envelope, Corine," Aunt Bee told her one day, smiling. This was the first time that Corine had seen her friend smile since Mara was taken.

Corine looked down to see the name, "Shemara Denise Washington," written on the envelope.

"Annie, you're scaring me. You seem unusually happy. Talk to me, Annie," said Corine.

Aunt Bee smiled. "I can go in peace now. Mara's going through. I can feel it, but the Lord let me know, He's going to send her some angels," said Aunt Bee.

"An angel? One angel?" Corine asked.

"No, angels, Corine, more than one. But, there will be a 'special' one. Mara's not going to suffer always. God assured me of that. Remember that song I taught Mara when she was just a baby? Send me an an-gel..." Aunt Bee sang.

"Yes, I remember it," Corine told her. "That was her favorite song. You said the Lord told you these things?"

"Yes, Corine. I had a vision earlier today when I was asleep."

"Annie..."

"Don't Annie me, Corine, I know what I'm talking about," Aunt Bee said, sounding serene. "The Lord can speak to any of us, however or whenever He wants to. I know it was real. It was very real! It is time I get my house in order."

"Annie..." Corine looked at her longtime friend.

"Corine, I want you to know how much I love you, girl. We've always been like sisters. You and I have been through so much together. God couldn't have blessed me with a better friend," said Annie.

"I love you, too, Annie," said a tearful Corine.

A week later, Aunt Bee died. Corine took her best friend's death extremely hard. She blamed Michael Washington for Annie's death. Corine knew that Mara was her life.

"God knows best," Reverend Wells told Corine. "Michael Washington didn't kill Sister Jackson. God took her, Corine. There is a difference. Michael doesn't give life, nor can he take life. God won't put anymore on us than we can bear. That is why it is so very important that God be our life, not humans. We love our family and dear friends very much, and we should love everyone as God has told us, but human beings should never be 'our life.' God should be the forefront and center of our lives, not man, not money, not material things. I know you're going through terrible times, Corine. I will keep you in my prayers. I'll keep little Mara in my prayers, also."

Aunt Bee requested in her will, that Mara's favorite song, Send Me An Angel, be sung at her funeral. Her favorite soloist, Chemese Craig, sang the song beautifully.

A beautiful poem, *A Road We All Must Cross*, was read by the pastor's daughter...

"A road we all must cross, and this is very true. Tomorrow is not promised to me, nor is it promised to you. Someday there will be a gathering, for you and I. For as surely as we live, one day, we will also say good-bye. No one knows the time, when they will leave this world. You can be richer than rich, you can have diamonds and pearls. Jesus Christ, God Almighty, is the One who makes the call. Not for rich, poor, black or white, but for all! Our hearts are very heavy. There is great pain! Some may ask themselves why, man will usually try to explain. It does not take the ill, nor does it take the old, the decision is made by HE, who sits high upon the throne. No matter what some may say, despite what some have been told, not only Sister Jackson, but we all must cross this road. As Jesus told Mary, 'Mary don't you weep,' Sister Jackson is not dead, she is only, asleep. God bless you, Sister Jackson, and may you rest in peace!"

*****

"Amen! Amen!" said the congregation, as they gave the pastor's daughter a thunderous applause.

Aunt Bee had been a member of the House of Prayer of the Apostolic Faith for over forty years. She was also very active in her community.

"Very beautiful and true poem!" said Reverend Wells. "Very beautiful!"

"Amen!" said the congregation again.

"Every time there is a 'Home Going,' it reminds us, yet again, how truly precious, and short, life is. Death can be on the doorstep, or around the corner, for any of us. And while it is important to give people their flowers while they are alive, it is more important, to make sure that your soul is saved! Make sure that you are right with God. That, is more important than anything! No human being knows when they are going to leave this world. Life is a gift from God. To be living, is a blessing. It is the biggest blessing of all. Live each day as if it were your last, because it just might be," said Reverend Wells. "Sister Jackson will be greatly missed. Our hearts and prayers go out to all of her family and close friends. We all loved her! God bless her soul. May she rest in peace."

Aunt Bee's last request was that a photo of Mara be placed inside of her coffin to be buried with her. Corine gave the photo to one of the pallbearers. She watched as he placed the picture inside her dear friend's casket.

Corine touched Annie's coffin for one last time. "Rest in peace, my sister," she whispered through her tears. "Rest in peace." God only knew, how badly, she was going to miss Annie.

There was a deep, newfound hate for the man who had caused so much heartache and pain, Michael Washington.

"When am I going back to Aunt Bee's?" Mara asked her father. "It's been a long time. I miss her a lot."

"Enough, Shemara! I'm tired of you asking me about Annie!" her father yelled.

"But, Daddy! You said..." Mara began to cry.

Her father went upstairs. He returned holding a large extension cord.

"Turn around, Shemara. I'm going to give you something to cry for!" Mike yelled, as he grabbed his daughter by her arm.

"I'm sorry, Daddy! I'm sorry! I won't ask anymore!" cried Mara.

"Shut up and turn around!" yelled her father again.

"Please! Don't hit me with that! I'm sorry, Daddy. Dad-dy! Please! I'm... I'm... sorry..." Mara cried.

"You will be sorry! Turn around! Turn around, Mara! Right now!"

The little girl finally turned around. It seemed the beating went on endlessly.

"Please, God! Please make him stop! Daddy..." Her father beat her until blood came from her body.

"Now, go to your room! Go to your room right now! Don't ever bring up Annie's name in my house, ever again!" said her father.

Mara could only crawl towards her room. She didn't feel her legs underneath her. Aunt Bee didn't spank her often, but the few spankings she did get, Aunt Bee always used a belt, and she would always spank her on her bottom. Mara had never been beaten before. Her entire body felt limp. She felt as if she were going to die.

"Get out of my sight, Mara! You're disgusting!"

"I'm mov-ing... I'm go-ing... Dad-dy," Mara said, faintly.

Michael phoned Natalie. "Hi, Nat. Yes, sure. I'm on my way. Wear something nice." Michael hung up the phone, then he turned and looked at Mara. "I have to go. I'm taking Natalie out to dinner. If this phone rings, you better not answer it! You hear me?"

"Yes, Dad-dy," cried Mara.

Mara never made it to her room. There was no way that she could climb up those stairs. She didn't have the strength.

Mara lay in a corner of the living room in a fetal position. She fell asleep humming her favorite song, Send Me An Angel.

****

When Mara awoke hours later, her father had not come home yet.

Mara walked slowly to her room, where she sat, looking out the window. It was dark outside. She could see the stars in the sky. She had always loved watching the stars. They were so beautiful.

Mara wondered what her aunt was doing now. Nine times out of ten, thought Mara, her aunt was sleeping. She knew that it was very late, and Aunt Bee always went to bed early.

Mara sat for hours, listening for the front door. If her father came home, she had already decided, that she would get in bed and pretend to be asleep. She didn't want another brutal beating.

Mara continued watching the stars in the sky. Her eyes kept falling on one particular star, because it was the most beautiful of all. It was that star, upon which, she made a wish.

## *Chapter Six*
## **Send Me An Angel**

Hunger and pain woke Mara in the wee hours of the morning. Her entire body was throbbing with pain. Mara began to cry when she saw her hands and arms. They were badly bruised, discolored, and swollen.

"Why did Daddy do this to me?" Mara cried. She was hurt inside, too. Mara did not understand why her father had beaten her, especially so brutally. What had she done? She never would have thought in a million years, the father she'd always known, or thought she knew, would do this to her. I hope I don't die. I hope he doesn't kill me, Mara thought to herself. She had never been so hurt and frightened in her life. I'll be really, really good from now on. I don't want him to do this to me again.

Mara's stomach kept growling. She was very hungry. She walked to the kitchen. The only thing Mara found in the kitchen to eat were some crackers.

"I'll eat those. I don't care what I eat. I'm hungry," she said aloud.

Mara placed some crackers on a plate, poured herself a glass of water, and sat down on the floor to eat. "Uh-oh, I forgot to say my grace."

It was three o'clock in the morning when she heard her father unlocking the front door. Mara got up quickly and ran to her room. Running made Mara feel worse, but she didn't have a choice. She couldn't let her father see her. Her intention was to stay out of harm's way.

"Daddy's home! Mara! I bought you some Cornflakes. You're probably asleep," said Michael Washington.

Mara wasn't asleep, she was afraid to speak. She did not want to say or do anything that might upset her father. Just hearing her father's voice now, made her heart beat rapidly.

Mara hoped that her father wouldn't come to her room. She would never forget the look in her father's eyes as he beat her. She never wanted to see that look again. Mara breathed a huge sigh of relief when her father didn't come to her room.

****

It was very difficult for Mara to fall asleep. She was in so much pain, and she was still very hungry.

Mara thought of Aunt Bee. How she missed her aunt! They had so much fun together. Mara hadn't seen her aunt in months. She wondered if Aunt Bee was still in the hospital. Mara hoped she was doing much better now. She wanted to ask her father about Aunt Bee, but after being beaten, she knew that she couldn't. Mara was very confused. She thought her father loved Aunt Bee, too.

Daddy can take away my words, but he cannot take away the love that I have in my heart for Aunt Bee, Mara thought.

"Aunt Bee," Mara whispered in the dark. "I love you!"

The next morning, Mara was awakened by the doorbell.

"Natalie!" she heard her father say.

"Hi, Mikey," said Natalie.

"What a nice surprise! Come on in," Mike said.

Natalie walked in and looked around the home. "Very nice, Mikey. Very nice. Where's that little runt of yours?" Natalie asked.

"She's in her room. Shemara! Mara! Someone's here to see you!" her father yelled. Mara winced as she walked slowly down the stairs. She was still in so much pain. "Mara, it's Natalie."

"Hi, there," Natalie said, looking at Mara as if she were a monster. "What happened to you? Are you dressing up early for Halloween?"

"No," said Mara, trying hard not to cry. Her feelings were deeply hurt. What a cruel thing to say, thought Mara.

"Don't get me wrong, Shemara, is it? It's obvious that you're a very pretty girl. I'd kill for your features, minus the bruises and swellings. Honey, you told me you spanked her, you didn't tell me you tried to kill her! Look, I simply came by to meet the little runt. I have to get home so Jennifer can do my hair. Mike, I will see you, later?" said Natalie, as she continued to stare at Mara.

"Of course, you will see me later. I have a full day planned for us. Wait, I have an idea! Why don't you and I go to Tiffany's for breakfast? Jennifer will wait for you. You know she will," said Mike, as he looked at his watch.

"Okay, I'll go wait in the car. Don't be long. 'Bye, runt," said Natalie.

"Mara, I'm taking Natalie out to breakfast. I bought you some Cornflakes last night," said her father.

"Thanks, Daddy."

Mara went to the bathroom to wash up. Afterwards, she came back downstairs to fix herself a bowl of cereal. She looked in the refrigerator. "Daddy, there's no milk," said Mara, looking at her father.

Mara's father walked over to her and slapped her hard, twice, across the face. Mara's bottom lip was torn and bleeding.

"Look what you made me do!" her father yelled. "You better not get any blood on my carpet either. Go clean yourself up! You kids today are so ungrateful! Some kids don't even have cereal to eat, and here you are whining about milk! And stop that crying! Now!"

While Mara walked to the bathroom to clean herself up, her father poured the box of Cornflakes on the floor.

"Mara!"

"Yes, Dad-dy?"

"I want every last flake picked up before I get back. You Denise looking... You're disgusting! You can eat them off the floor for all I care! You're an animal anyway! And remember, don't answer the phone," said her father. "Do you hear me, girl?"

"Yes, Dad-dy..."

Mara picked the cereal up off the floor. She had to eat the cereal. There was nothing else in the house to eat. She had already eaten all of the crackers.

Mara's hands were trembling, and her entire body was shaking. She had never been so frightened in her life.

"Her mother must have been a real looker!" said Natalie, when Mike got in the car. "Where is her mother?"

"In the grave! I killed her," Mike said, coldly.

"You can't be serious. You're kidding, right?" Natalie asked, looking at Michael Washington in disbelief.

"Of course, Nat. Please, talk about something else."

Natalie sat beside Michael in silence. She was very interested in Mara and her mother.

Natalie didn't believe Michael when he told her that Mara's mother was dead. Perhaps Mara's mother was unfit, and Mike had won custody of their daughter. But then again, from the looks of things, he was also unfit. Poor child, thought Natalie.

Natalie couldn't get the enormous fear that she saw in the little girl's eyes out of her mind. Shame, thought Natalie. She's such a pretty little girl. She remembered the smooth skin, the long dark brown hair, the cheekbones... Natalie could only imagine that whenever Mara did smile, her smile must be very pretty, also.

Although Natalie had never wanted children of her own, she still didn't like seeing anyone being mistreated, especially a little child who was helpless. If Mike abuses his own daughter, thought Natalie, am I next? She couldn't help but wonder.

When they arrived at Tiffany's, Natalie found that she was no longer hungry. Her appetite had disappeared completely. Natalie couldn't get Mara's face out of her mind. She was sorry that she had been so cruel to Mara. There was nothing funny about abuse or neglect.

Michael Washington came home hours later. "Mara?" He knocked on her bedroom door. When there was no answer, he opened it. "Mara?"

The little girl stirred. When her father saw her swollen face and bottom lip, he immediately applied ice on both.

"Make sure you keep ice on your face and lip. School starts soon," said her father. "You don't want to scare the other kids," added her father with a laugh.

Mara was deeply hurt by her father's abuse and comments. She was very scared and nervous around her father, too.

Every day and throughout the day, Mara's father applied ice and cocoa butter on her face and lip. After two weeks, the swellings and bruises had almost disappeared, but the scars inside of the young girl, still remained.

Mara couldn't wait for school to start. She was tired of being beaten by her father. She was also tired of being hungry. Mara had lost weight since she began living with her father.

Mara liked it much better when her father wasn't home, since this was the only time, she did not walk around in fear.

Mara would sing her favorite song every day. "Send me an an-gel... send me... send me an an-gel..." Mara would sing her heart out. Never before did Mara mean those words as much as she did now. She prayed that God would hear her, and answer her prayers. This was one time in her life, that Mara knew, she really, needed, an angel.

Mara stayed in her bedroom most of the time watching television. Her all time favorite TV show was *The Brady Bunch*. Mara also enjoyed *Good Times*, *Happy Days*, *The Flintstones*, *The Waltons*, and *Charlie's Angels*.

And every day, without fail, Mara would count down the days. School couldn't start fast enough for her.

After all, thought Mara, if Cindy Brady, (her favorite character on *The Brady Bunch*), enjoyed school, she knew that she would enjoy school, too.

Mara practiced writing her name and numbers every day. She could count to one hundred, thanks to Aunt Bee, who had taught her. Her teacher was going to be very impressed by what she knew, thought Mara, smiling.

Hours later, Mara stood looking in her closet. Her father had bought her so many clothes that she could wear a different outfit every day for the entire school year. She had plenty of shoes, too.

Mara had picked out the outfit that she was going to wear on her first day of school, weeks ago. She'd hoped by doing that, it would make time go faster.

Mara did many things for herself now, including combing her hair. She had finally convinced her father to let her comb her own hair. She hated it when her father combed it. Mara laughed at the thought. She would always look like a "Martian" girl with her two long pigtails standing straight up. "Earth to Mara" is not what she wanted to hear from the other kids at school. Mara had no intention of using her pigtails as radars. If she were trying to connect with Martians, they may have come in handy then, but that wasn't the case.

Mara continued to look at all of her beautiful new clothes and shoes. Her heart immediately grew sad. She would have traded all of it to be with Aunt Bee again, to be with someone, who loved her.

"Sometimes it's not the things that you do have, but the things that you don't have, that counts the most." Tears fell from Mara's eyes, as she remembered her aunt's words.

****

The first day of school finally arrived. Mara was overjoyed!

"Mara, remember what I have always told you, my golden rule, anything that goes on in the Washington's house, stays in the Washington's house," said her father, in a threatening voice.

"I remember, Daddy," said Mara.

Michael Washington smiled to himself as he took Mara to class. He had a reputation to live up to. He was a well-known attorney. Mike wanted to appear to be a great father, too. Appearing to be a great father would make him look good in the public eye.

Now that Mara would be going to school, her father thought as he walked back to his car, he would have to refrain from hitting her in areas that could not be covered up. Michael Washington also knew that child abuse laws were very stringent now.

"Do they serve dinner here?" Mara asked a teacher standing in the hall after her father left.

"Well, something similar," said the teacher. "You will eat breakfast and lunch here. You'll eat dinner at home."

I might not, Mara thought to herself. It would depend on how her father was feeling.

Mara stood and watched children being brought to class by their parents. Some of the children seemed nervous; others appeared to be just as happy as she was. Mara saw some mothers crying. She smiled and greeted everyone who walked through the door.

Mara was very happy. School had finally arrived! And no one was happier, than Shemara Washington.

## *Chapter Seven*
## **The Revelation**

Time passed quickly. Mara had been going to school for almost two months now.

School was a breath of fresh air for Mara. She had not been beaten or yelled at here. Well, with the exception of the encounter with the "bully giants," then her good friend, Lilla Belle, had come to her rescue. Mara had always been able to eat at school, too.

Miss Monner was right. Education IS very important. Mara learned a lot during her first few months at school.

She wished that she could share what she learned with her Aunt Bee. She knew that her aunt would be very proud of her!

Lilla Belle and Ivana were another reason that Mara enjoyed school so much. They were her best friends. They did many things together.

Mara's only regret about school, so far, was that she could not live there.

Although it was fall, it felt like summer. The weather seemed to get hotter and more humid every day.

One day during recess, even Mara agreed. "It's hot!" said Mara, and without thinking, she pulled up her sleeves.

"Mara!" Lilla Belle and Ivana said at the same time.

"What happened to you, Mara? How did you get all of those bruises on you?" Lilla Belle asked.

"I fell," Mara said, pulling her sleeves down quickly. "I'm always falling." Mara tried to laugh it off. "Clumsy me!"

"Mara," Ivana said, looking at her seriously, "you're far from clumsy."

Tears filled Lilla Belle's eyes as she stood looking at Mara. She didn't know who, but she knew someone had hurt her friend very badly. She liked Mara a lot, and like Ivana, Mara was like a sister to Lilla Belle.

"Mara, those bruises are... I'm going to go tell Miss Monner," said Lilla Belle.

"No! Lilla Belle, I told you I fell!" said Mara.

"Mara..." Ivana said, agreeing with Lilla Belle. "I think Lilla Belle's right. I think we should tell."

"I don't think we should tell, Ivana, I 'KNOW' that we should tell!" said Lilla Belle.

"If either of you were my friends, you wouldn't tell!" said Mara, looking frightened and angry.

"Mara, if we weren't your friends we wouldn't tell, but we are your friends. That's why we're going to tell! I'm going to tell the teacher," Lilla Belle said again, as she left to tell Miss Monner.

Miss Monner was standing by the swings with the other kindergarten teacher, Mrs. Adkinson.

"Miss Monner? I need to speak with you in private, please," said Lilla Belle.

"Certainly," said Miss Monner, walking to an area where no one was standing. "What is it, Lilla Belle?" the teacher asked, looking curious.

"It's... it's Mara."

"Yes? What about Mara?" Miss Monner asked.

"I think someone's hurt her." Lilla Belle explained.

The teacher walked quickly towards Mara and Ivana. "Lilla Belle and Ivana, I'd like to speak with Mara in private, please," Miss Monner told them. After both of the girls left, Miss Monner asked Mara to pull up her sleeves. "It's okay, Mara. I'm here to help. May I see, please?" the teacher asked. "May I?"

As Mara slowly pulled her sleeves up, Miss Monner looked on in shock.

"Oh, my God!" said the teacher. "Mara! Who did this to you? Come with me, Mara." Miss Monner took the little girl's hand. "Marilyn, please watch my class."

"Sure, Betty," said Mrs. Adkinson.

Miss Monner took Mara to the nurse's office. Once they were inside, she closed the door behind them. The teacher explained everything to Beverly Green, the school nurse.

"I think it's a good idea to get Mable in here, too," said the nurse.

Mable Williams was the school counselor. Mable came immediately; her office was only two doors down from Beverly's.

The nurse examined Mara, thoroughly. Her entire body was badly bruised, some areas were even swollen.

There were no signs of sexual abuse. All three ladies knew these bruises had not occurred from falling, as Mara continued to state.

"Call the police!" said Mable.

The nurse and counselor left to talk privately in the next room.

"Who do you think did this to her?" the nurse asked the counselor.

"I don't know, but my guess would be a parent. This is a young child. What parent wouldn't notice such awful, discolored bruises on his child's body?" Mable went on, "Mara's clearly very frightened. She doesn't want to tell, probably due to fear of retaliation. That's very common though. Let's see how she reacts to her father when he arrives."

"Are you calling her father?" Beverly asked.

"No. I will let the police do that," said Mable, as she joined Mara and Miss Monner in the nurse's office again.

The police came immediately. Coincidentally, Officer Banks, one of the same officers that arrived when Mara's mother had called the police years ago came, along with Officer Gilmore.

"Washington? That name sounds so familiar," Officer Banks said aloud. However, he knew there were many people with that last name. Officer Banks didn't think anymore of it until he heard his partner ask for Michael Washington.

"I'm sorry. He's about to leave for court. May I take a message, please?" Michael Washington's receptionist asked Officer Gilmore.

"I need to speak with him now," Officer Gilmore insisted.

"Sir, who are you? And, what is the nature of your call?" the receptionist asked.

"I'm Officer Gilmore. I work for the Beaver Creek Police Department. I need to speak with Mr. Washington, now, ma'am," the officer said, firmly.

"Hold, please," said the receptionist, as she placed Officer Gilmore on hold for several minutes. "Thanks for holding, sir. I'm sorry, but Mr. Washington really does need to leave for court now."

"Well, tell him we can come get him out of court, or he can get on the phone now," said Officer Gilmore, not taking no for an answer.

"Hello!" Michael Washington said angrily.

"Mr. Washington? You need to come to your daughter's school, immediately. We have a problem. A very serious problem."

"What part of the English language do you not understand?" yelled an angry Michael Washington.

"Excuse me?" said Officer Gilmore.

"What is it? I don't have time now! I'll have to come when I'm finished in court," said Mara's father.

"I suggest you make time. It's not an option. See you soon, Mr. Washington," said Officer Gilmore, hanging up the phone.

Michael Washington arrived at Jones Elementary a short time later.

"What's this about?" he asked, looking at the police officers, Miss Monner, his daughter, Mable, and Beverly.

"Your daughter's body is badly bruised. Some areas are even swollen. You mind telling us how the bruises and swellings got there?" Officer Banks asked.

"Bruises? Swellings?" Mara's father asked, looking and sounding surprised. "Mara is five years old. Kids get bruises all the time! I had plenty of bruises when I was her age."

"You haven't even looked at the bruises, Mr. Washington," Officer Banks pointed out.

"Yes, you're right. What was I thinking?" said Michael Washington, walking towards his daughter.

Mara flinched when her father reached for her. The counselor and nurse looked at each other.

"It's okay, honey. Daddy's here, let me take a look." Mara flinched again. "Those are awful bruises! Mara, you're going to have to be a lot more careful!" her father said, pretending to be a doting father.

"But I... I didn't tell them anything, Daddy!" Mara cried. "Daddy, I didn't..."

"What are you talking about, sweetheart?" Michael asked his daughter.

"We meet again, Mr. Washington," said Officer Banks.

"I don't remember you," said Michael Washington.

"I remember you quite well. Think back, roughly, five years ago. Ring any bells?" said Officer Banks.

Officer Banks stopped there. He didn't want to discuss what had happened in front of Mara. The officer remembered that Mara's mother had given birth to her, then died shortly thereafter.

And now, a five-year-old Mara sat before him, almost as badly bruised as her mother had been years ago. It took everything Officer Banks had in him to refrain from striking Michael Washington. He wanted to kill him.

"Michael Washington, I'm placing you under arrest. Place your hands behind your back. You have the right to remain silent. Anything you say, can and will be used against you in a court of law. You have the right to an attorney. If you cannot afford an attorney, one will be appointed to you by the court."

"You're making a big mistake! Do you know who I am?" yelled Michael Washington.

"I know what you are! Get him out of here!" Officer Banks told Officer Gilmore.

Miss Monner stood, looking at Michael Washington as if seeing him for the first time. She never would have thought this man would be capable of doing such a cruel and awful thing to a poor, innocent child. The saying never judge a book by its cover is so very true. Miss Monner thought of all the times Mike Washington appeared to be a caring, loving father when he'd picked Mara up from school. The teacher shook her head sadly. You just never know.

Miss Monner and Beverly left Mara and the counselor alone. Mrs. Williams told Mara what would happen now. She even told her a joke. She was happy to see the little girl laugh.

"Mara, Gloria Wilson, will be coming to pick you up. She works for C.P.S., Child Protective Services," Mrs. Williams explained. The counselor also told Mara that she would be visiting her on a regular basis. "It is very important that you receive counseling because of the horrific experiences that you have been through. I will never try to force you to talk about what happened," said the counselor. "It is important that you go at your very own pace. Here is my card. My home phone number is on this card, too. If you need or want to talk to me, if you are being mistreated. Call me for anything. It doesn't matter what time or day it is either," said the counselor. "I do have voice mail, so if I am not there, please leave a message. Again, I will be checking on you often. You will be seeing a lot of me. Remember, Mara, you are not alone. Okay?"

"Okay," Mara replied.

When Gloria Wilson arrived, Mable and Gloria spoke privately in Mable's office about what had taken place. Afterwards, Mara left with Gloria.

"Are you hungry, Mara?" Gloria asked.

"Not now," said Mara. "Thanks anyway."

Mara sat in silence as Gloria drove her to the foster home. She was very scared and curious about many things. Mara feared retaliation from her father, most of all, but there wasn't anyone that she felt she could talk to.

"Mara? Are you all right?" Gloria asked. The little girl's eyes were full of fear.

Mara nodded her head. "Yes, Mrs. Wilson."

Mara kept thinking. What is going to happen to me now? How long am I going to stay at that place? What is living in a foster home going to be like? Am I going to like it there? Will my dad be able to get me again? That was her worst fear of all. She was certain that her father would kill her if the courts put them back together again. That thought made Mara shudder.

"Mara, everything is going to be all right," said Gloria. "I'm going to take excellent care of you."

Mara had always affiliated foster homes with unwanted kids. That's exactly what I am, thought Mara. Nobody wants me.

When the school bell rang to go home, Lilla Belle and Ivana told Mrs. Wongley about Mara. They asked if they could go check on her before going home.

"Sure," said Mrs. Wongley.

Lilla Belle and Ivana led the way to the counselor's office, as Lea Wongley and Zach followed.

****

"Mrs. Williams? Is it okay if we see Mara?" Lilla Belle asked the counselor.

"I'm sorry, but Mara's left already," said Mrs. Williams.

"She's left? Where is she?" Ivana asked.

"Because of privacy reasons, I'm not at liberty to say. However, you can both write her. I'll make sure she gets your letters. I'm sure your parents won't mind helping you write Mara. I will also ask her to call you ladies. Would you both like that?" Mrs. Williams asked Lilla Belle and Ivana.

"We sure would!" said the girls in unison.

The counselor's phone rang. "Excuse me. Hello, Mable Williams speaking."

"Hi, Mable, it's Gloria. Can you talk now?"

"Let me switch this call to Bev's office. You mind holding?" the counselor asked Gloria.

"Not at all, Mable, go ahead," Gloria replied.

"I'm going to have to take this call in Bev's office," said the counselor. "You'll are welcomed to sit and wait for me. I won't be long."

"Mom, may we? Please!" Lilla Belle looked at her mother with pleading eyes.

"Sure, sweetheart, we'll wait," said Lea Wongley.

****

"Now, where were we?" the counselor asked when she returned.

"Numbers, Mrs. Williams. We're going to write down our phone numbers, so that you can give them to Mara, so that she can call us. Day or night," said Lilla Belle.

Lilla Belle and Ivana wrote down their phone numbers and gave them to the counselor.

"Can you tell us if Mara's coming back to school and if she's going to be all right?" Lilla Belle asked again. She was very concerned about Mara.

"I certainly believe that Mara is going to be all right," said Mrs. Williams. Especially now, thought the counselor.

"Is she ever coming back?" Ivana insisted.

"Girls, Mrs. Williams has already told us that she's not sure if Mara's coming back," said Lea Wongley.

"There is one thing that I am certain of," said Mrs. Williams.

"What's that?" asked Lilla Belle.

"Mara has two great friends!" said the counselor.

****

That night at dinner, Lilla Belle thanked her parents.

"Thanks for what, sweetheart?" her mother asked.

"Thanks for loving me and Zach. And thanks for not abusing us," said Lilla Belle, thinking about Mara.

"You're welcome, Lilla Belle," said her father. "We love you two very much. We would never hurt you."

"Thanks for talking to us, also," said Lilla Belle. "Without you'll talking to us about abuse, I wouldn't have known what to do about Mara. I just might have saved her life. I hope so, anyway."

"Lilla Belle, thank you, for listening," said her mother.

****

Mara sat alone in the room assigned to her by Mrs. Wilson.

"This will be your room for now," Mrs. Wilson told Mara.

No one wants me, Mara thought sadly to herself. She sat on her bed, thinking about what was going to happen to her now. She didn't know Mable Williams or Gloria Wilson that well, but so far, neither of them had beaten her, or yelled at her. Both ladies were very nice to her. Mara wondered how long that would last.

Days passed. For some reason, Mara felt very comfortable with Mrs. Williams. She asked the counselor if her father would be able to come and get her.

"You would have to help us with that, Mara. Your father was arrested. He's out on bail now, but he is also going to court. As of now, there is a temporary restraining order against your father," said the counselor. "He cannot come to get you now. The decision will be made by the jury at the end of your father's trial. To prevent that from happening, if he in fact, did this to you, I hope that you testify. That will certainly make a difference. A big difference."

"Mrs. Williams? Can I live with my Aunt Bee again?" Mara asked, her eyes were filled with hope.

"Mara, there is something that I need to tell you. Your aunt..."

"My aunt? What about Aunt Bee?" Mara asked. She remembered her father telling her that

Aunt Bee was in the hospital for surgery several months ago. Mara had not seen or heard from her aunt since then. There was not a day that went by that Mara didn't think of her Aunt Bee.

"Mara, your aunt... Aunt Bee died." The counselor knew that there was no easy way to tell the little girl.

Mara began to cry. "Why didn't anyone tell me? What happened to her?"

"I don't know why you were not told before now. I'm not even sure your father knew. I found out last night, along with Mrs. Wilson and Miss Monner. That's one of the reasons I came to visit you today. I told them I would tell you. I don't know what caused your aunt's death," said the counselor.

Mara was devastated! Aunt Bee was the only person who really loved her, Mara thought sadly to herself, and now, she was gone. She... was gone, and she would never come back, ever!

Mara loved her aunt so much. Mrs. Williams held little Mara in her arms, as she cried and cried. The counselor stayed with Mara for a long while. She knew the little girl needed someone to comfort her.

Mara wished she knew why her aunt never wrote, called, or visited her. But now she felt that she would never know.

"Aunt Bee was the only person who really loved me!" cried Mara. "And now she's gone!"

The counselor hugged Mara. "I love you, Mara. And God loves you, too!" said Mrs. Williams.

After Mara fell asleep, the counselor left.

Mrs. Williams had a long talk with Gloria before leaving that evening. Their hearts went out to the little girl. They both hoped things would get much better for Mara.

## *Chapter Eight*
## **A Change Is Going to Come**

Mara never played with the other children at the foster home. Everyone was nice to her, she'd told Mrs. Williams. Mara started opening up to the counselor more and more.

But nothing made Mara happier than receiving letters from her two best friends, Lilla Belle and Ivana. Mrs. Wilson would always read the letters to her. She would also assist Mara with writing Lilla Belle and Ivana back. Lilla Belle even sent her money. They were such true friends! It saddened Mara that she would never see them again.

Mara often wondered about what was going to happen to her. She had been in foster care for weeks now.

There were several positive things that Mara experienced in foster care: not being beaten and being able to receive consistent meals. Mable Williams and Gloria Wilson seemed to care a lot about her, too.

A young couple came to visit Mara one day. They seemed to like her a great deal. Mara really liked them, too.

Gloria became very happy, because she was hoping the couple would adopt Mara.

Gloria had seen many children come and go, but for some reason, she had a special fondness for Mara. She was such a sweet little girl. Mara was also very well-mannered.

Gloria knew the loneliness and fears were still there. Mara didn't trust people, and from all that she had been through, this was not only normal, but clearly understandable.

Mable Williams was doing an excellent job with Mara. She was the best counselor that Gloria had ever seen.

Mara finally told Mrs. Williams and Judge Sanders, the judge presiding over her case, that her father had indeed abused her. Mara told them that he left her home alone and left her without food, many times. She also told them that her father never wanted her to use, or answer, the telephone.

Mara testified, via video, in the judge's chambers. She feared testifying in court with her father watching her. The judge was very understanding.

The Washington's next door neighbor, Mrs. Brewster, also testified. She told the jury that she heard Mara scream in horror many times.

"I should have done something!" said Mrs. Brewster, crying. "I'm doing something now. I was afraid. My husband would tell me to mind my own business. We were both afraid to say anything to Mike. He even left the little girl home alone, many times, even late at night."

"How do you know that?" Judge Sanders asked Mrs. Brewster.

"His girlfriend, Natalie Simms, told me, Your Honor. We're not close. I first met her through my daughter who works with her. I'm here to do what I should have done a long time ago. I'm here to help little Mara." Mrs. Brewster began sobbing again. "Natalie would talk about that little girl, as if the things that Mike did to her were funny. I believe 'runt' is what she called the little girl."

The judge remembered Mara telling him that her father's girlfriend called her "runt."

"Thank you, Mrs. Brewster. I have no further questions," the state attorney told her. He was very pleased with her testimony.

Judge Sanders looked at Michael Washington's attorney. "Mr. Palmer, do you have any questions for Mrs. Brewster before she steps down from the witness stand?"

"No, Your Honor, I do not."

"What do you mean you don't?" Michael Washington yelled in outrage.

Judge Sanders rapped his gavel. "Mr. Washington! Another outburst like that, and I will have you removed from my courtroom! Do you understand me?" said Judge Sanders, looking at Michael Washington.

"Yes, Your Honor, I'm sorry. It won't happen again," said Michael.

"It had better not happen again." Judge Sanders gave Michael a stern look.

Michael Washington's trial was short. Natalie even testified. It was another devastating testimony for Mike. Natalie's conscience had been eating at her since day one. Like Mrs. Brewster, she felt guilty, too. They were all guilty, almost as guilty as Mike, thought Natalie. The little girl could have been killed. Natalie finally did what she knew was right.

****

On November 9th, Michael Washington was asked to stand to hear the reading of his verdict.

"We the jury, find the defendant, Michael John Washington, guilty, for child abuse and child neglect. We hereby sentence you to ninety-nine years in prison, without the possibility, of parole. The defendant is to be taken into custody, immediately."

A very visibly shaken Michael Washington stared at the jury. He was led out of the courtroom, this time, in handcuffs and leg irons.

Judge Sanders was very happy that the "rich" did not escape justice this time. He had seen too many times when the affluent went free.

The judge didn't let Natalie or the Washington's neighbors, the Brewsters, off the hook either. The threesome received a $25,000 fine, four years of probation, and two thousand hours of community service doing volunteer work at a local child abuse center.

"I am appalled by the three of you," said Judge Sanders. "A little girl's life was in danger, and your excuse is, that you feared for your own lives, and it was not your business. Saving a life, is everyone's business. Fear is no excuse. Imagine what little Mara was going through. I'm sure that she was considerably more frightened than any of you were. There are too many ways and options to remain anonymous when reporting any crime, therefore, saying that you were afraid, is clearly no excuse. It is no excuse whatsoever. There are many children who have died, and they might have lived, if the abuse were reported by people who knew about the abuse. It's the same thing with domestic violence. How many more lives must we lose? As with any crime, everyone of us, MUST get involved! Abuse is a highly increasing and ongoing problem, that is costing many lives. Try placing yourselves in Mara's shoes. You are all being fined and punished because you broke the law, by knowing about the abuse, and not reporting it. Abuse is very serious. It's life threatening, and it often leads to death. Let this be a lesson to all of you." Judge Sanders rapped his gavel.

Gloria and Mable were pleased with the judge's decision to fine and punish Natalie and the Brewsters. They were extremely pleased with Michael Washington's verdict.

"He won't be able to hurt Mara ever again," Gloria said to Mable, who was sitting beside her in the courtroom. Both ladies breathed a huge sigh of relief when they heard the verdict.

The counselor hoped the Washington case would send a very strong message to other parents and child care providers who abused and neglected their children. How could some people be so cruel and heartless?

The counselor thought of the many people in the world who desperately wanted children but could not have any. She also thought of the people who could and did have children, but abused, neglected, or even killed them. Mrs. Williams shook her head sadly.

Both ladies cried when they saw the photos of Mara's body that were displayed in the courtroom. All of the jurors had cried, too. It was by the grace of God, that little Mara was still alive.

"I'm very happy the jury prosecuted Mara's father to the full extent of the law," Gloria told the counselor.

Mable nodded her head in agreement. "So am I, Gloria, so am I!"

Later that day, Gloria received a phone call from the Chandlers. They were the young couple who had showed a lot of interest in Mara.

"Mrs. Wilson, I'm sorry, we would love to adopt little Mara..." Mrs. Chandler paused. Gloria sensed a "but" coming.

"But... my heart is really set on a newborn," Mr. Chandler finished.

"Okay," said Gloria, looking over at Mara. Both she and Mara had been waiting on the Chandlers' call. Mara was eager and ready to go. She had been talking about it all day.

"Mrs. Wilson? Are the Chandlers running late?" Mara asked, after she saw Gloria hang up the phone.

"Mara..." Gloria's eyes said it all.

Tears filled Mara's eyes. "You don't have to say anything. I can tell by the look on your face. They don't want me. No one wants me! I'm going to turn in early, Mrs. Wilson."

"Mara..."

"It's okay, Mrs. Wilson. I'd like to be alone for a while," said a tearful Mara.

"Sure, honey. I'm here if you need me," said Gloria. "You know that, sweetheart."

Mara nodded her head. "Yes, Mrs. Wilson, I know. Thank you."

Gloria watched as Mara walked to her room. Her heart went out to the little girl. "Please... God, send Mara a family who's going to love her and take excellent care of her. Please, God," said Gloria. "Please."

When the mailman arrived, there was a letter for Mara from Lilla Belle. Gloria smiled. She knew the letter would lift Mara's spirits. Speaking of perfect timing, thought Gloria.

"Mara, you have a letter from Lilla Belle!"

Mara smiled through her tears. "Will you read it to me please, Mrs. Wilson?"

"Sure, sweetheart," said Gloria.

"Dear Mara,

How are you doing? I hope fine. I am doing okay. School's okay. But, it is not the same without you, Chick. Seriously, Mara, Ivana and I miss you a whole lot! We were like the Three Musketeers. We had a lot of fun together, didn't we? Mara, how are things going with you? Keep your head up, keep smiling! Things are going to be just fine. I have to think about Grandma Ella's words. She says that God can do anything! She also says that He will do things, however He sees fit. I'm an optimist, so I believe that, too. According to the dictionary, an optimist is simply a person who always hopes for the best possible outcome. I am expanding my vocabulary. How am I doing so far? Zach, Grandma Ella, and Webster, help me a lot! Anyway Mara, my brother is helping me write this letter. Zach is smart, too. But he's not as smart as me, or you. (Smile). I am drinking a glass of water. A little water got on the letter and smeared it. But, it's okay. I will still be able to get this letter in the mail today.

*Write back soon! And take care, Mara!

L.Y.L.A.S. (Love You Like A Sister!)

-Lilla Belle Wongley

*P.S. Mara, I don't know if you've ever noticed or not, but I am left-handed, just like you are! And guess what? Grandma Ella says that means that we are in our right minds! Here's some money for you; you can pay me back in thirteen years. You'll be eighteen then."

There was a smear on the letter because Lilla Belle had been crying.

The Wongleys knew their daughter had not been herself for several weeks now. Dolores told Lea that Ivana acted as if she had lost her best friend.

"Well, apparently she did. Apparently they both did," Lea told Dolores.

Lea Wongley awoke that night to her daughter's cries.

"Lilla Belle? What is it, sweetheart? Did you have a bad dream?" her mother asked.

"No, Mommie! Mommie, why can't Mara live with us?"

"Lilla Belle..."

"I don't mind sharing my things. Please! Mommie, please!" Lilla Belle cried.

"No, sweetheart," said her mother. "Calm down and get some sleep." Lea Wongley stayed with Lilla Belle until her daughter finally fell asleep.

Lea tossed and turned that night. She couldn't sleep after leaving her daughter's room. She turned the night light on beside her bed.

"Ben? Ben?" said Lea, shaking her husband.

"Uh-huh? Honey, what is it?"

"Ben, I need to talk to you."

Her husband opened one eye to look at the clock. "Two o'clock in the morning? Honey! Why can't it wait until a few more hours from now?"

"Because it can't," his wife insisted.

"Okay, sweetheart, I'm listening," said Ben.

"Ben, I wouldn't mind having another daughter."

"Lea, are we pregnant?" her husband asked.

His wife laughed. "No, Ben, we're not pregnant! I'm talking about Lilla Belle's friend, Mara."

"Yeah, the little girl who was abused by her father. That was horrible! Her father's an animal. The story has been in the media a lot lately." Ben knew that if Michael Washington wouldn't have been a well-known attorney, he wouldn't be on the news or in the newspapers, every day. But he was very happy that a monster like that was being exposed. "Lea, are you saying what I think you're saying?" asked a very sleepy Ben Wongley.

"Yes, Ben, I am. We need to make this decision as a family though. I already know how the children feel. And I know what my thoughts are. I know we can't save the world," Lea Wongley went on, "but we can make a difference. And it would be one less child in the world, who is being abused, neglected, or even killed. We should never let the fact that we can't help everyone, stop us from helping someone. What are your thoughts, honey? Are you sure you don't mind our adopting Mara?"

"Sweetheart, if I minded anything, you know that I've always told you. I will always be honest and upfront with you," Ben told his wife. "I do not say things that I don't mean, and I'm not about to start now. I will make some phone calls later this morning. I'll see what I can do."

"Thanks so much, sweetheart!" his wife said, giving him a hug and kiss. Lea knew that when her husband said he'd see what he could do, it was as good as done.

Mr. and Mrs. Wongley agreed not to say anything to anyone yet, especially the children, until they were absolutely certain that they could adopt Mara.

****

The first thing that Ben Wongley did later that morning was call Judge Sanders. "Judge Sanders? Hello, this is Benjamin Wongley."

"Well, well, well, it's been a long time, Ben," said the judge.

"Yes, it has," said Ben.

The judge remembered the very handsome man with the movie star looks. He and Ben went to high school and college together. Both men were Harvard graduates.

Ben met with his old friend later that morning.

"That's a mighty fine thing to do," said Judge Sanders, in his trademark southern drawl. "Mighty fine! You'll obviously have big hearts. I don't see why adopting Mara would be a problem. Do you think she'd want to become part of the Wongley family?"

"As far as I know, if Lilla Belle's on the moon, Mara would go there, too. And vice-versa. Lilla Belle and Mara are very close friends. Apparently, they are already like sisters. My daughter hasn't been the same since Mara left," said Ben Wongley.

"Well, I want nothing but the best for that little girl. She has been through more than enough hardships already," said Judge Sanders. The judge told Ben Mara's entire history, in detail.

"That's awful!" Ben exclaimed. "How soon can we get this done?"

"Just say the word," the judge told him.

"The word," said Ben, laughing. Ben called his wife to meet with him and the judge. Judge Sanders wanted to meet with both of them. Ben called their attorney, Sam Woods, after the meeting ended. "I want the legal documents drawn up immediately," Ben told Sam.

Mara's adoption papers were prepared and waiting for the Wongleys at the City Hall in Beaver Creek in the judge's chambers.

Judge Sanders agreed to meet the Wongleys and Mara in his chambers later that evening. For this event, the judge had gladly made an exception to work later than usual.

****

The Wongleys made plans to pick Mara up from the foster home; then they would go to City Hall where the judge and their attorney would be waiting for them.

Ben called the counselor, who'd been a godsend for Mara, to tell her the great news. Mable Williams was ecstatic.

Ben phoned Gloria afterwards. "Gloria Wilson, please."

"This is she," said Gloria.

Ben shared the news with her. "Mrs. Wilson?"

"I'm here, Mr. Wongley. I'm... words cannot express how happy I am. Mara's a beautiful little girl; she's smart, too," said Gloria. "I care a lot about Mara, Mr. Wongley. She's been through enough for several lifetimes."

"I know, Mrs. Wilson. Lea and I are going to take excellent care of Mara. We will treat her the same way that we treat Lilla Belle and Zach. I promise you that," said Ben.

"I certainly hope so, Mr. Wongley," said Gloria. Tears welled up in Gloria's eyes. "Mara deserves happiness! She's a great kid."

"I assure you, Mrs. Wilson, Mara will be in the best of hands. No family will love her the way that we will," said Ben.

After hanging up from speaking with Ben Wongley, Gloria was visited by Corine's daughter, Lori.

"Mother told me to make sure that if I ever saw Mara again, or knew where to find her, to make sure that she gets this," said Lori, handing Gloria an envelope. "Please. Be sure and give Mara the document that I've just given to you. Mother passed away a month ago." Lori paused because it was still hard for her to discuss her mother's death. "Aunt Bee and Mother, can both, rest in peace now," said Lori.

After Lori left, Gloria sat thinking about Mara's aunt. She had obviously loved that little girl very much. And Mara certainly loved her Aunt Bee a lot, too.

Gloria also felt that Michael Washington's taking Mara from her aunt played a large part in her aunt's death. She was certain of it. However, she never shared those thoughts with anyone.

"Mrs. Wilson, is everything okay?" Gloria's assistant asked her.

"Yes, Ashley, thanks. If things work out the way Mr. Wongley assured me they would, everything would be more than okay." Gloria told Ashley about the Wongleys' plan to adopt Mara.

"Wait a minute! 'The' Wongleys? As in mega-bucks, own the town Wongleys?"

"Yes, Ashley. 'Those' Wongleys. Mara needs love more than she needs money," said Gloria.

"Boss, I understand exactly what you're saying, but please hear what I'm saying, too. Money's not everything, it's the only thing! And money doesn't talk, Mrs. Wilson, it shouts!" Ashley joked.

"You are too funny, Ash!" said Gloria.

"And having a father who looks like Benjamin Wongley certainly doesn't hurt either. Very handsome, filthy rich, and very powerful. Not a bad combination, huh, boss?" said Ashley. Gloria only laughed in answer.

Gloria had been in great spirits after receiving the call from the Wongleys. She hoped nothing would stop the adoption from taking place.

She'd heard about this family. Who hadn't? They were the most prominent family in town. Wongleys and money were synonymous.

Gloria didn't know the Wongleys personally, but they seemed down-to-earth. She knew that they were very generous, too. They always donated money and time to help the less fortunate. They were also a family who seemed to have very good morals and values, and Gloria knew how important those things were.

Gloria had seen the entire Wongley family once on TV. Lea Wongley was very beautiful and elegant. She could have easily been a model. Zach was a "miniature" Ben. He looked exactly like his father. An exact replica, only smaller. And the little girl, the one that Gloria had heard so much about, Lilla Belle. She looked like both of her parents, which made for undeniable beauty. The Wongleys were, undoubtedly, a great looking family.

But regardless of their wealth and good looks, the most important thing the Wongleys could offer Mara, was love. Love that was unconditional!

Gloria sat smiling and thinking to herself, answered prayers, sometimes come in unexpected ways.

****

The Wongleys asked Talli, the children's babysitter, to pick them up from school and watch them until they returned home that evening.

Miss Monner and Mrs. Marcus called the Wongleys to verify this request, as this was school policy at Jones. The Wongleys had to fax a signed, authorized letter to Mr. Stavros, also. Parents' signatures were verified by signatures kept on file in the principal's office. Without all of these procedures being met, students could not get picked up by anyone, except their parents.

****

"How was everyone's day?" Talli asked Lilla Belle and Zach.

"My day was great, as usual," said Zach, with a big smile on his face.

"And yours, pretty girl? How was your day?"

"Okay. It was better when Mara was in school," said Lilla Belle.

"Mara?" Talli asked.

Lilla Belle nodded. "Yes. Mara was a little girl in me and Ivana's class. She no longer goes to Jones though."

"Did she move?" Talli asked. She had never seen Lilla Belle's eyes look so sad.

"It's a long story, Talli. I write her though. Ivana does, too," said Lilla Belle.

Talli wanted to ask more questions, but decided against it. Lilla Belle didn't seem up to going into details.

****

Mara said good night to Mrs. Wilson and turned in early as usual.

"Good night? Mara! It's only six-fifteen!" said Gloria.

"I know, Mrs. Wilson," said Mara.

"How do you know what time it is?" Gloria asked, testing Mara.

"Because the short hand is on the six and the long hand is on the three," Mara told Gloria.

"Wow, Mara! You're as smart as you are pretty. Good night, honey; call me if you need me," said Gloria.

Gloria looked at her watch. The Wongleys should be here soon, she thought.

Gloria hadn't told Mara about the document that Corine's daughter, Lori, had given her, nor did she tell Mara about the Wongleys' plan to adopt her. She didn't want to get the little girl's hopes up, only to break her heart once again.

Gloria remembered Benjamin Wongley's words. She felt that he was a man of integrity. Gloria also liked it when Ben told her that he'd be a great father to Mara, and that he would love and treat her the same way he treated Lilla Belle and Zach.

There's not a family in this world, who will love Mara more than we will, Ben had told Gloria again, before hanging up the phone.

Gloria smiled. She could hear in his voice that Benjamin Wongley was being truthful. She knew that Mara would be in very good hands, the best of hands, and that was very important to her.

****

"Gloria Wilson? Hello, I'm Benjamin Wongley. This is my wife, Lea," said Ben. The Wongleys shook Gloria's hand.

"Where is our little girl?" Mrs. Wongley asked.

"Oh, my! You'll are here to take her?" Gloria asked.

The Wongleys nodded.

Gloria led the Wongleys to Mara's room. "Mara, you have visitors!" a thrilled Mrs. Wilson told her. Gloria was very happy the Wongleys hadn't backed out.

"Visitors?" Mara asked.

"I'll leave you'll alone. I'll be in my office if anyone needs me," said Gloria, leaving the room.

Mara sat on her bed. She was very surprised to see the Wongleys at the foster home. She had specifically told Mrs. Wilson that she did not want any visitors. She felt ashamed being there. But at least the foster home was there for her and for all of the other children in need. And for that, Mara was very grateful. Aunt Bee had always told her to be grateful.

"There is always someone worst off than you. Believe it or not," Mara remembered Aunt Bee saying.

Mara made a pact with herself to always use and keep the great values and teachings that her aunt taught her. She knew that would be a good way to make her aunt proud of her. Aunt Bee would always be in her heart. She would always be with her in spirit, too. Mara turned her attention back to the Wongleys.

"Mr. and Mrs. Wongley? Did Lilla Belle ask you'll to come here? I wrote her back. Tell her and Ivana that I'm hanging in there," said Mara.

The Wongleys smiled in answer.

"First of all, Mara, I need to give you this," Lea Wongley said, handing Mara the document that Mrs. Wilson had given her.

Mara recognized the handwriting instantly. Her dark eyes lit up. "Aunt Bee's handwriting!" said Mara, excitedly. Mara opened the envelope. "I'm not that advanced yet. Would one of you please read this to me?"

"Sure, sweetheart," said Mrs. Wongley. "It says...

*My Dearest, Precious, Mara,*

*I love you so very much! I will always love you. I don't have long here. I told Corine I knew that you were going through something terrible. I could feel it! When you're close to someone, you can often feel things. I called so many times. Your father would never let me speak with you. He did everything he could, to keep me out of your life. Mara, you will always have a very* special place in my heart, not even your father or death, can keep us apart! When you get this letter, I feel your angels will have arrived, even that "special" angel, that God told me about. The good Lord always keeps His promises! I pray that God, and His angels, watch over you, ALWAYS! After all, no one can watch over you the way that God can. I love you so very much, sweetheart! Your mother, Denise, loved you dearly, too. Enclosed is a photo of her. Now, you can see where you got your good looks from! MARA, always remember, WE LOVE YOU, DEEPLY, FOREVER,, AND ALWAYS!

-Aunt Bee!"

Mara was very happy! All of her questions had been answered. Aunt Bee still loved her!

"You'll always be in my heart, too, Aunt Bee," Mara said aloud. "ALWAYS!" Mara stared at the photo of her mother. "She was very pretty," said a tearful Mara.

"She sure was," said the Wongleys in unison.

"She was gorgeous!" said Mrs. Wongley. "You look just like her, sweetheart."

Mara was even more angry at her father. He had obviously hurt Aunt Bee a lot, too. Mara still had not been told how her mother died. The counselor told the Wongleys this was not a good time to tell her.

"Mara's been through so much already, and she's still very young. There is so much that she still does not understand. It ultimately depends on how well she continues to do in therapy," the counselor told the Wongleys, earlier that day. "Mara has certainly made progress. Let's take one step at a time, one day at a time."

Mrs. Williams told the Wongleys that she would be visiting Mara on a regular basis. She also told them that Mara would receive regular, visual check-ups. The counselor made it very clear that she was not going to assume anything. This was also one of the numerous orders from Judge Sanders. The Wongleys understood and agreed.

They couldn't wait to break the news to their children. They'd decided to surprise the children, especially Lilla Belle. Although they knew that their son would be very happy, too.

Lilla Belle had taken Mara's situation very hard. Ben and Lea Wongley often admired the great characteristics that they saw in their young daughter.

Many children wouldn't care about another child's heartaches, but Lilla Belle cared a great deal. She was wise beyond her years, and she had such a big heart!

Ben and Lea thought about both of their children. They were so very proud of them.

The Wongleys vowed to give Mara plenty of love, attention, support, and parental guidance. They would give her everything that they gave Lilla Belle and Zach.

After reading the letter, Lea Wongley placed it back in the envelope. She then hugged Mara, who was still crying and holding her mother's photo.

"It's all right, sweetheart. Everything is going to be all right," said Benjamin Wongley. "Especially now."

"Thanks for coming to visit me," Mara told Mr. and Mrs. Wongley. "I wrote Lilla Belle and Ivana. Will you'll give them these letters, please?"

"No, Mara, actually we won't," said Ben Wongley.

"No? Okay," Mara said, looking surprised.

"Mara, I said no, because you're going to give them the letters yourself," said Ben Wongley.

"I can't. I don't want them to see me here," said Mara.

"How would you like to become a member of the Wongley family?" Lea Wongley asked Mara.

"Lea and I would love to have another daughter," said Ben Wongley.

"And Lilla Belle and Zach would love to have another sister, too," his wife added.

Mara was silent. She kept looking from one to the other, trying to see if Mr. and Mrs. Wongley were serious.

Mara's eyes lit up. "Are you'll serious?" she asked. "REALLY serious?"

"We sure are!" said the Wongleys.

"We're very serious!" said Ben.

Mara was overjoyed, and then that same, sad, familiar feeling came over her.

"What's wrong, sweetheart?" Lea Wongley asked. She could tell by the look on Mara's face that something was wrong. She hoped the little girl hadn't changed her mind about becoming a part of their family. "Mara, what is it?"

"My father... I was so happy with Aunt Bee and he took me from her. He almost killed me, too. He beat me senseless. I don't want that to happen again." Tears streamed down her tiny cheeks.

"I promise you, Mara, your father will never hurt you again," said Lea Wongley. "Now, do you think Lilla Belle would go for that?" Mara laughed through her tears, as she shook her head no.

"And neither will we!" said Benjamin Wongley. "Your father is going away for a very long time. And he deserves what he got and more! I know what he did to you, sweetheart. It was horrible! I promise you, I will never let him, or anyone, hurt you. You don't have to be frightened anymore. Don't worry about your father, Mara; I'm your father now. I'm not your father by blood, but I'm definitely your father by love. And that's the best relation of all. You will not have to worry about Michael Washington hurting you, ever again. You won't even have to worry about him getting the chance or opportunity, to hurt you again," Benjamin Wongley assured Mara. "You have my word, sweetheart."

****

"We'd better get going. Someone has been wanting to see you!" said Mrs. Wongley, looking at her watch.

"I'll be right back!" Mara exclaimed. She ran to Mrs. Wilson's office. "Mrs. Wilson! I have great news! The Wongleys are going to adopt me! They are going to adopt me! I'm going to be a part of their family!"

"That's fantastic, sweetheart! I am so happy for you! You deserve the best, Mara. I'm going to miss you!" Mara gave Gloria Wilson a big hug. Tears of joy filled Gloria's eyes.

"Thanks for being so nice to me, Mrs. Wilson. I'm going to miss you, too. May I use the phone, please?" Mara asked.

"Sure, Mara," said Gloria.

Mara called Mrs. Williams, to whom she had also grown very close. She had memorized the counselor's phone number. Mara shared the great news with Mrs. Williams.

"That's wonderful, Mara!" Mrs. Williams told her. "I'll see you next week."

Mara thanked Gloria again, then she quickly returned to her room where the Wongleys were anxiously waiting for her.

The Wongleys and Mara, happily and quickly, packed all of her belongings.

Mara couldn't stop smiling. Unbelievable! Who would have guessed? Mara was elated to be going home with the Wongleys. She knew that she was going to be loved and cared for. She would not be beaten or starved, and she would never be alone. There was no question about that. Mara could already see the love that Mr. and Mrs. Wongley had in their eyes for her. The little girl hadn't seen that look since she last saw her Aunt

Bee. It's so wonderful to be loved, thought Mara. Fantastic!

As they drove to City Hall, Mara's thoughts were on Lilla Belle. She had been with her through thick and thin.

The letters that Lilla Belle wrote her, made her day; they were always very encouraging. Mara still had the money that Lilla Belle sent her. I might keep it. After all, Mara smiled, I do have thirteen years to pay her back. And Mara felt certain that she could make that deadline. In her heart, Mara knew what Lilla Belle had done for her was priceless. She knew that she could never repay her.

"God sent me an angel," said Mara, who couldn't stop smiling. "Lilla Belle!"

The Wongleys and Mara arrived at City Hall, shortly after leaving the foster home.

Judge Sanders started the proceedings immediately. “Shemara Denise Washington, it is my understanding that you wish to be adopted, and that Benjamin and Lea Wongley wish to adopt you, also.”

The Wongleys and Mara said “yes” to the judge and nodded their heads. The attorney and Judge Sanders carefully reviewed the adoption papers again.

Afterwards, Judge Sanders asked the Wongleys to sign the adoption papers. He then had their attorney witness it.

“Do I need to sign, too?” asked a very happy Mara.

Everyone laughed.

“No, young lady, you don’t have to sign,” said the judge, still laughing.

Judge Sanders smiled at the little girl. He had never seen Mara so happy. His heart went out to her. There was light at the end of the tunnel. The judge knew that all cases didn’t end happily as Mara’s did.

“I hereby declare, by the power vested in me by the State of Texas, that Shemara Denise Washington, is the lawful daughter of Benjamin and Lea Wongley, adopted this nineteenth day of November. Mr. and Mrs. Wongley, you can now officially change Mara’s last name, too, if you wish. Congratulations!” Judge Sanders rapped his gavel.

“I will take care of the name change right away,” Sam told the Wongleys.

****

Judge Sanders stood, smiled, and shook hands with everyone, including little Mara.

Mara was very happy! She was going to be living with her best friend, who was now officially, her sister.

The Wongleys knew that they had touched a little girl's life in a big way! So did Judge Sanders, who could not stop thanking them.

Lea Wongley thought again of her young daughter, Lilla Belle, and how she sparked all of this.

The Wongleys took Mara by the hand and led their daughter to the car.

"Let's go home, ladies!" said Ben. "Zach and I are really in trouble now. Three ladies!"

Lea Wongley and Mara laughed in answer.

****

Ben entered the house first. "Hello, Talli. Where are the children?"

"Hi, Mr. Wongley. The kids are in bed," Talli answered.

"Good! Thanks for coming through for us once again, Talli," said Ben, handing her a check for babysitting.

Ben then beckoned for his wife and Mara to come inside of the house. Mr. and Mrs. Wongley led Mara upstairs. They told her to wait in the hallway.

"Lilla Belle! You'll want to wake up for this!" said her mother.

"Hi, Mommie and Daddy. Where have you'll been?" Lilla Belle asked, rubbing her eyes.

"Someone is here to see you!" Ben told his daughter.

"Who?" asked Lilla Belle.

"Come on in, little one!" said Lea Wongley.

"Mara! Mara! Oh, my! Mara! Oh... wait... Mommie and Daddy, is she..."

"A Wongley?" said Zach, who'd been eavesdropping in the hallway. "You betcha!"

Lilla Belle hugged Mara and cried. Zach hugged them both. He hated to see his sisters cry, even if it was tears of joy.

Lilla Belle held Mara for dear life. She couldn't believe that Mara was actually in her house. In her bedroom! And the biggest shock of all, Mara, was now, her sister!

Ben and Lea stood watching Lilla Belle. They had never seen their daughter so happy.

"Hear ye! Hear ye!" said Zach. "On the count of three, we will sing, Lilla Belle's Song! One-ee, two-o-oo, three-ee..."

Mara sat and listened to the words of the song.

***"Lil-la Belle! Lil-la Belle! She's the bravest little girl in the whole wide world! Whole wide world! With a heart so big and a smile so bright; no matter what happens she will stand by your side! Lil-la Belle! Lil-la Belle! With long black hair, and eyes that shine, she's pretty as can be and she's oh so wise! Lil-la Belle! Lil-la Belle!"***

"Now, it's my turn!" said Lilla Belle. "I'm glad that I did tell! I'm glad that I yelled! I'm glad they put that monster under the jail! Under the jail!" Lilla Belle sang.

Those words couldn't be more truthful either, thought Mara, who knew that Lilla Belle was talking about her father.

Mara looked at Lilla Belle with love and admiration. She had done so much for her. Mara chuckled, as she remembered her encounter with the bully giants. Lilla Belle had bravely stood up to the bully giants, for her. Mara didn't know it at the time, but Lilla Belle, was the angel, who was going to change her life, forever.

God's angels come in all different sizes, shapes, and colors, thought Mara. She knew that her aunt was looking down on her, smiling. Aunt Bee was right, her "angels," had arrived!

Mara smiled, knowing in her heart, that she was going to be very happy and safe here.

"Welcome to the family!" said Lilla Belle, as she gave Mara another big hug. "Mara, your initials will still be, S.W., Shemara Wongley!" Everyone laughed. "Mommie, Daddy, I can't thank you'll enough!" Lilla Belle looked at her parents lovingly, smiling at them, through her tears. She couldn't remember when she'd been so happy. "Change can be good!" said Lilla Belle.

Benjamin Wongley looked at his wife. And, as if reading her father's mind...

Lilla Belle said, "Grandma Ella told me that. Change CAN be good!" Lilla Belle said again. "VERY, VERY GOOD!"

**For more **INFORMATION on**:

*__**Child Abuse,**__ please **call:**
**1-800-4-A-CHILD / (1-800-422-4453)**

***__Domestic Violence__:**
**1-800-799-SAFE / (1-800-799-7233)**

Michelle Cole is currently working on her upcoming novel, **F.A.T. Chance**.

*You may e-mail Ms. Cole at:

**Inccole@cs.com**

Dear Readers:

I hope that you enjoyed reading this book, as much as I enjoyed writing it!

Best wishes!

-*M. C.*

Printed in the United States
1011700003B